"I want you, Megan," he whispered.

His honeyed words trickled through her body like warm water. Her hands gripped his arms. In that instant his mouth clamped over hers. It was firm and possessive, a reassurance that took away all her fears and common sense at the same time. Meg knew this was mad, dangerous and totally wrong, but for once in her life she didn't care. She simply relaxed into his embrace and let his passion engulf her. It was far too wonderful to resist, but she knew she had to make a token effort.

"We can't, Gianni. *I* can't."

Sliding one hand beneath her chin, he lifted her face. First he placed a kiss on the tip of her nose. Then the need to kiss her properly again overwhelmed him.

Meg was powerless to stop him, and when he lifted his lips gently from hers a second time he murmured, "Of course we can. When I show you how good it can be you'll never want another man."

CHRISTINA HOLLIS was born a few miles from Bath, England. She began writing as soon as she could hold a pencil, but was always told to concentrate on getting a "proper" job.

She joined a financial institution straight from school. After some years of bean counting, report writing and partying hard, she reached the heady heights of "gofer" in the marketing department. At that point, a wonderful case of love at first sight led to marriage within months. She was still spending all her spare time writing, and when one of her plays was short-listed in a BBC competition, her husband suggested that she should try writing full-time.

Half a dozen full-length novels and a lot of nonfiction work for national magazines followed. After a long maternity break, she joined a creative writing course to update her skills. There she was encouraged to experiment with a form she loved to read but had never tried writing before—romance fiction. Her first Harlequin Presents title, *The Italian Billionaire's Virgin,* began life as a two-thousand-word college assignment. She thinks that writing romance must be the best job in the world! It gives her the chance to do something she loves while hopefully bringing pleasure to others.

Christina has two lovely children and a cat. She lives on the Welsh border and enjoys reading, gardening and feeding the birds. Visit her Web site at www.christinahollis.com.

THE COUNT OF CASTELFINO
CHRISTINA HOLLIS

~ Her Irresistible Boss ~

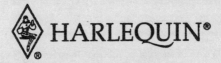

HARLEQUIN®

TORONTO • NEW YORK • LONDON
AMSTERDAM • PARIS • SYDNEY • HAMBURG
STOCKHOLM • ATHENS • TOKYO • MILAN • MADRID
PRAGUE • WARSAW • BUDAPEST • AUCKLAND

Recycling programs
for this product may
not exist in your area.

ISBN-13: 978-0-373-52774-8

THE COUNT OF CASTELFINO

First North American Publication 2010.

Copyright © 2009 by Christina Hollis.

This edition published by arrangement with Harlequin Books S.A.

For questions and comments about the quality of this book please contact us at Customer_eCare@Harlequin.ca.

www.eHarlequin.com

Printed in U.S.A.

THE COUNT OF
CASTELFINO

PROLOGUE

MEG could hardly believe her luck. Charity Gala Night at the world-famous Chelsea Flower Show, and she was part of it! The rich and famous jetted in from all over the world for this exclusive preview. Her display of tropical flowers attracted them all, so she was getting a grandstand view of their wealth and beauty. When she heaved a sigh now, it was only to experience the fragrance of a million flowers and acres of crushed grass. Her career might be on hold, but this experience was taking her mind off her pain.

Suddenly, a strangely determined movement caught her eye. A gorgeous man was threading his way between the tycoons and movie stars. Patting a shoulder here, kissing a woman there, he looked as though he owned the place. Tall, athletic and moving with natural grace, he was born to wear a tuxedo. Meg couldn't help following him with her eyes. His dark good looks were illuminated every few seconds by a flashing smile as yet another person tried to catch his eye. Meg wondered what it would be like to be part of his charmed circle. Watching him was her window into another world. When the crowd closed around him, hiding him from view, a light definitely went out of her evening. She dropped her gaze to the reality of her job on the Imsey Plant Centre stand again, wondering what it would have been like to sample some of his charm for herself.

The expression froze on her face as she realised her daydream was about to come true. Her ideal man was walking straight towards her display stand, and smiling. He obviously wanted to attract her attention. He got it—instantly.

'Buona sera, signorina!' He twinkled, his voice rippling with Italian delight. 'I need beautiful presents for some…*special* people. I've been told this sort of plant is foolproof…' he continued, looking down at an open notebook in his hands. Frowning briefly, he raised his eyes to hers again with a particularly devastating smile. 'Mmm…I wonder—can *you* read this handwriting?'

He made no move to hold the little book out to her. Meg couldn't reach it from where she stood. She might never get a better chance to approach a man like this. Glancing apprehensively all around, she nipped around the end of the Imsey stand and went to his side. She felt unbelievably shy, but it was worth it. The closer she got, the more darkly handsome he became. He wasn't just lovely, he had everything. His designer suit was so crisp and new, a gold Rolex shone against his flawless tan, and when he moved she was engulfed in a waft of expensively discreet aftershave.

'This is the first chance I've had to get out from behind this display all day, sir!'

'Don't worry. I'll make sure it's worth your while.'

With a flutter of pleasure, Meg heard all sorts of unspoken promises in his voice. It didn't take a mind reader to know that was exactly what he intended. Smiling down at her indulgently, he showed her his notebook. The first thing she noticed was the way his fingers curled around its leather-bound cover. They were long, strong and a shade of brown more usually seen on the men who worked beside her in the greenhouses at home. There was only one difference. Unlike them, this man had fingernails that were neat and clean. Meg found herself wondering if the rest of him was equally smooth and perfect...

Her handsome customer cleared his throat. It was a soft, polite sound but Meg's guilt made her jump. She looked back at his notebook. Most of the page was covered in staccato Italian written in a strong, clear hand. Then an expansive, old-fashioned script had added something. Meg leaned close to her visitor, trying to make out what it said. The warm night released another tantalising hint of his expensive cologne into the air. She inhaled, trying to make it sound as though she were concentrating. This was a once-in-a-lifetime moment for her. When she had served him, this stunning man would be gone from her life for ever. Meg made sure she stretched out the moment for as long as she could.

'It's an Imseyii hybrid, sir. They're exclusive to my family's nursery,' she announced, leaning back from him with regret. She was rewarded with a look that made everything worthwhile. His dark brown eyes glittered with pleasure. Meg gazed into them, and was lost. His teasing smile was as irresistible as the rest of him and she felt herself getting warmer by the minute.

He leaned toward her with a wicked grin. 'What I want to know is: *do women like them*?'

'They can't resist them, sir!' Meg giggled, surprising herself. She had never found anything remotely funny about her work before. 'Our orchids are the perfect impulse gift to give a lady.'

'Or perhaps *several* ladies?'

Meg let his remark pass. There were too many people relying on her, back at home, for a flirtation to lead her astray. Turning away from the influence of his beautiful eyes, she spread her hand towards her display, inviting him to admire the carefully crafted arrangement she had made of the nursery's best plants. Dozens of them nestled in a bed of soft green moss. Hundreds of arching stems as fine as florist's wire trembled in the slightest movement of air. Each was set with dozens of perfect little flowers, some plain, some patterned, and in almost every colour of the rainbow. Meg was so proud of them she allowed herself another smile.

'They're often called "dancing delights". Are you tempted, sir?'

Her handsome customer put his head on one side and looked at her mischievously. 'That depends. Do you dance?'

Meg giggled again. At any other time, in any other circumstances she would have cursed herself for being so unprofessional. Tonight, it felt *right*. Simply looking at this man lightened her heart. There was something about the glitter in his sloe-dark eyes, and the life burning in his expression.

'I don't suppose you need to dance, with a smile like that.'

Magically, the gap between them closed. Meg couldn't see him moving, but it was definitely happening. Confused, she looked at her plants. 'I don't have time for dancing, sir—or anything other than nursery work, really. Looking after all these is more than a full-time job...'

'Then you must do it very well. Everything is looking lovely.' He tilted his head again, and there was no mistaking his expression.

'Thank you!' Meg responded with a delight that overcame her shyness. And then she realised he wasn't concentrating on the plants, but on her. Immediately a molten core of heat threatened to melt every square inch of her skin. It erupted in a blush as he trained a knowing look straight at her.

'I'll take a dozen. Send them around to my Mayfair apartment. That should keep my current string of beauties quiet for a day or two. My name is Gianni Bellini. Here's my card, and thank you—these last few minutes have been a real pleasure.' His smile was roguish, and told Meg that plants definitely took second place with him. 'Now, I must pay.' He pulled out a sleek leather wallet and extracted a sheaf of banknotes along with his business card. As he passed them over to her a smile animated his beautiful lips and suggestive eyes. Her blushes flared again as he took her hand in his warm, sure grip. Raising it to his lips for the soft sensuality of a kiss, he reduced her legs to jelly.

'And so, until the next time we meet, *mio dolce…*'

Dark eyes flashing, he nodded a discreet farewell. Then before Meg could gasp or laugh or speak, he withdrew his touch, turned and vanished into the crowds…

CHAPTER ONE

MEG woke with a jolt and realised she was back in her aircraft seat. Her heart tumbled thirty thousand feet. A lot had happened since the Chelsea Flower Show, but the image of Gianni Bellini still haunted her. Only the thrill of starting work full-time at the Villa Castelfino could take her mind off him. She had been commuting to Tuscany regularly over the past few weeks, but from today she could properly call herself the Count di Castelfino's Curator of Exotic plants. It was the official start of her new job with her grand Italian employer. Although she was looking forward to it, Meg was very nervous. It was the first time she had lived so far away from her parents, and she didn't like leaving them to cope with their business alone. It didn't help that after sleeping on the plane she had a head full of cotton wool, and all the most uncomfortable bits of her aircraft seat imprinted on her body.

Shuffling off the plane along with everyone else, she comforted herself with the thought someone would be waiting for her in Arrivals. Once she left airside, Franco the chauffeur would be there to help with her luggage, as usual.

Meg's budding self-assurance lasted for as long as it

took her to glance around the waiting area. Franco was nowhere to be seen. With a flicker of fear she wondered if this meant there was trouble at the Villa Castelfino. She had picked up enough from working alongside the Count di Castelfino to know that the old man did not get on with his son. Meg had never seen *il ragazzo*, as her aristocratic employer scornfully called his heir, but she had learned enough to dislike him. The Count di Castelfino loved the varied landscape of his estate with its olive groves, gnarled oaks and wildflower meadows. His son wanted to transform it into a monoculture—nothing but ordered rows of vines as far as the eye could see. As for the count's beloved plant collection—Meg smiled ruefully to herself. Life at the Villa Castelfino sounded like a continuous struggle between beauty and business. The old man's hobby was always in danger of losing out to his son's ambition.

She waited and waited, but no one arrived to collect her. It was a bad start for someone with half a ton of luggage. Time crawled past. Looking up and down the concourse, she spotted an arrow pointing towards a taxi rank. Rather than wait and worry, Meg swung into action. Pushing her trolley towards it, she waited nervously for a vacant cab, glancing in every direction. Neither help nor trouble arrived, but by the time she could scramble into the safety of a taxi she was in a state of nervous collapse.

The driver recognised the address she gave him, and let fly a delighted stream of Italian. Meg went weak with relief. At last something was going right. She tried to explain her situation, but soon used up her tiny vocabulary of halting holiday phrases. Her driver found the whole thing hilarious. Unable to understand and feeling totally isolated, Meg sank back in her seat.

I wonder what gorgeous Gianni is doing right now. Not being stood up at an airport terminal, that's for sure! she thought, imagining him shouldering aside his flock of girl-friends to rescue her. She sighed, wondering if she would ever see him again. It didn't seem very likely. Her only hope would be to persuade the Count di Castelfino to stage an exhibit of his plants at one of the big London flower shows. In her dreams, the gorgeous Gianni Bellini haunted them in search of more treats for his harem.

She spent the taxi ride imagining what it must be like to be seduced by such a charmer. *It's no wonder he's got so many girls in tow,* she thought. His smile had warmed her in a way she hadn't experienced for a long time. She was strictly a one-man girl, so common sense always told her to put a lot of distance between herself and men like Signor Bellini. But a wisp of wicked excitement curled through her daydreams like smoke. In her fantasies, she could do what she liked.

And so could Gianni…

While Meg simmered, the man of her dreams stared down the barrel of a gun. It might look like the neck of a crystal decanter, but it was equally deadly. Gianni Bellini knew full well that alcohol solved nothing. It would only slow him down. Going for so long without sleep was bad enough, and drinking would only make it worse. It would have a knock-on effect on him, and all his newly inherited staff, for the rest of the day. He decided against it.

'Shall I fetch you some champagne instead, Count?' A uniformed waiter bowed obsequiously. All he got in reply was a grunt and a dismissive wave of his new master's hand.

Barely twenty-four hours into his life sentence, Gianni was still coming to terms with what had happened. He had known this would be his destiny for as long as he could remember. Reacting by developing a strong streak of independence, he had made sure he didn't have to rely on his inherited wealth. Instead he had forged a brilliant career for himself. While his father was alive, Gianni's Castelfino vineyard had been relegated to a distant corner of the estate. That was about to change. Now Gianni was in total control, his business would take centre stage. Despite his exhaustion, he smiled. That would stop the questions, for a while at least. People knew he was obsessed with the idea of making Castelfino wines a luxury with an international reputation. They would think he was simply shelving any quest for an heir while he expanded his empire.

Now he had inherited all his father's land and property, there would be no stopping him. Every suitable inch of the Castelfino estate would be turned over to growing grapes. Production would rocket, and so would Gianni's sense of satisfaction. He enjoyed playing the part of self-made millionaire, although his playboy image was a pretty intangible asset. It was good to have a new girl every night, but they were nothing more than a perk of the job. While celebrity spotters tried to guess which one of his beautiful companions would be chosen to produce the Bellini heir, Gianni kept his real love a secret. The Castelfino vineyard was his baby. When it came to children…Gianni didn't want anything to do with them. His own childhood had been made an absolute hell by his warring parents. He couldn't stomach the idea of inflicting that on an innocent infant.

A movement outside the summer dining room caught

his eye. In the far distance a dust devil spiralled along the line of the drive. It was heading for the villa. Gianni's eyes narrowed with annoyance. He really didn't need visitors right now. With an exclamation, he slid his palms back across the white linen of the tablecloth and cranked himself to his feet. His sleep-deprived brain was still functioning, but his limbs were set in concrete. Crossing the room, he went out through the open French doors and onto the terrace. However he felt, he had a duty to those arriving to pay their respects to his late father. He shut his eyes, concentrating on what he would say.

The Tuscan countryside sounded as only an afternoon in high summer could. In the still, hot air not a leaf moved. A single bird called, with the monotonous *chip-chip* of two parched stones tapping together. The only other sound was that single car engine, making a tunnel through the dense air as it tore towards him. Everything else held its breath.

Gianni heard the car swing around in an extravagant semicircle to stop in front of the villa's main door. Puzzled, he opened his eyes and saw—not some grand limousine, but a simple radio cab. There wasn't time to be shocked before its driver bellowed a hearty greeting and leapt out to open the car's boot.

The cabbie began hauling out suitcases and piling them on the dusty ground, while keeping up a cheerful conversation with his still invisible passenger. Gianni stared at the scene with disbelief. All the time the car radio chattered away. No one at the Villa Castelfino had raised their voice above a whisper for days. Until that moment, the vast face of the house had been blank with shutters closed against the sunshine. Now flickers of movement ran along behind many of them. This unexpected racket was mobilising

Gianni's staff. Sure enough, one of the kitchen lads raced out from a side door to tackle the new arrivals. While he was busy silencing the cab driver, the brand new count got another shock.

The rear door of the taxi opened and the most beautiful woman in the world struggled out. Her skirt, already short, had ridden up during her journey exposing long, beautifully shaped legs. Her dark blonde hair moved loosely around her shoulders, shining in the sunlight. She looked dazed. As she straightened up she staggered slightly, as though pushed back against the security of the car. Gianni realised she had been caught off guard by the sudden contrast between the air-conditioned taxi and the sun-baked amphitheatre in front of the Villa Castelfino. *Is it any wonder,* he observed, *when she's wearing tights?*

With a curse, he turned away. His body had sprung to life as it always did at the sight of a pretty girl. How could it possibly play a tasteless trick on him like that, today of all days? A keen interest in all things feminine was only natural, but noticing such fine detail at a time like this was grotesque. Gianni dropped his gaze to his feet. And then he heard her laugh. It was as captivating as a charm of goldfinches.

'Signor Bellini! What a surprise! I never expected to see you again, let alone here! What a lovely surprise!'

He heard her take long, confident strides toward him across the gritty forecourt. From his vantage point on the terrace he could look down on her with the mere flick of a glance. As she noticed his bitter, twisted expression she stopped smiling. In half a dozen steps she went from delight, through puzzlement, to concern. Her steps became hesitant, and when she spoke again her voice was halting and uncertain.

'You *are* the man I met at the Chelsea Flower Show, aren't you?'

'*Sì*. I am Gianni Bellini.'

He dropped the words like icicles, but then recognition swept over him. This was the flower girl. Gianni never forgot a pretty face—or a curvaceous body like hers. Manufacturing a smile, he nodded a brief welcome. Details slowly came back to him. This one was not only beautiful, she was clever, too. That was enough of a novelty for her to have made a special impact on Gianni at the time, but he had never dreamed of seeing her a second time.

The force of his reply didn't stop her. She advanced with another laugh and stuck out her hand in greeting.

'Good grief, I never would have believed it. You've changed—all those girlfriends must be running you ragged, *signor*!'

'What are you doing here?' he enquired in a voice like cut glass. As he spoke he looked down at her outstretched hand as though he would rather shake a viper by the tail.

She frowned, looking into his face as though searching for recognition.

'I work for the Count di Castelfino. I'm moving into the Garden Cottage today. Someone usually meets me at the airport, but for some reason the chauffeur didn't turn up today.'

'That is because my father is dead. I'm the Count di Castelfino now,' he announced with crisp formality.

Her smile vanished, and she stared at him in growing horror.

'Oh…I'm so sorry.' Helplessly she looked from the taxi, to her heap of suitcases and then back to him. 'How crass of me to arrive in such a flurry like this… C-can I ask what happened?'

'He suffered a stroke some days ago, in Paris. He died yesterday—*no*, the day before—'

Shaking his head, Gianni raised one hand and dragged it wearily down over his face. The rasp of stubble under his palm was loud and intrusive in the horrible, thick silence.

'I—I'm so sorry…' she repeated, her voice soft and insubstantial.

Exactly like her, Gianni thought instinctively, before silently cursing his reactions again.

'You weren't to know. I didn't know you were expected. That's why no one was sent to meet you. I was only driven back here an hour ago.' Distracted, he looked across at the taxi and pulled out his wallet. 'I'm afraid you've had a wasted journey. You'll have to go back to wherever you came from. How did you get past my security guards at the gate, in any case?'

Her eyes opened wider and wider as he spoke until they looked like two clear reflections of the cobalt sky.

'They were expecting me…my name is on today's visitor list…so they just waved my taxi straight through…' Her voice was faint. As it faltered still further he had to lean closer to hear what she was saying. 'But I can't go back…all the plants here will need someone to look after them. The count—the *old* count—would have wanted them cared for properly…'

Gianni shook his head. 'I'm the Count di Castelfino now, and I have my own plans. It's the start of a new regime. There's no room here for anything that doesn't pay its way. Whatever projects my father may have had in mind won't be going ahead. I'm in charge now, and my interests are much more practical.'

As he spoke he saw the heaven of her eyes become cloudy and misted with tears. She shrank visibly, and when she spoke her voice was barely more than a whisper.

'You can't mean that, *signor*?'

'I'm afraid so. The Castelfino vineyard is my only concern. I'm interested in practical projects, not hobbies.'

Springing lightly down from the terrace, he started to walk towards the taxi. Because old habits couldn't be shaken off, he put a comforting arm around her shoulder to lead her in the same direction. 'Don't worry, *signorina*. I'll pay your taxi fare back to the airport. By the time you get there, my staff will have phoned through and arranged a return ticket for you. Where did you fly from, by the way?'

'Heathrow—but—'

As they reached the open passenger door of the taxi Gianni took his arm away from her. After pressing far too much money into the taxi driver's hand, he swivelled on his heel and walked off. As he headed back to the villa he threw a few disjointed words over his shoulder at her.

'I'm sorry you've had a wasted journey, *signorina*. Goodbye.'

Closing a mental door firmly in her face, he forced himself to push thoughts of her inviting full lips and big blue eyes right to the back of his mind. He ought to be concentrating on his plans for Castelfino Wines, not distractions like her.

And then a voice interrupted his thoughts, ringing out through the hot, still air.

'No, thank you, Signor Bellini.'

He stopped and frowned. That wasn't supposed to happen. If the girl was going to say anything at all, it should have been a diffident 'yes'. That was the way things worked in Gianni's universe. People did what he told them to do. While he stood wondering how she could possibly have misunderstood his instructions, he heard a muffled bang. It was followed by the sound of light footsteps in the dust. That made him look back, over his shoulder. What he saw puzzled him still more. The girl had dropped her hand luggage and was running to catch him up.

Gianni Bellini, Conte di Castelfino, thought of all the staff members who would be watching this fiasco from behind the Villa Castelfino's shutters. They all knew his reputation. The old place must be alive with gossip already. Playboy he might be, but Gianni knew what to do. It wouldn't hurt to reinforce his authority. When this girl launched her screaming, hysterical scene, he would silence it with a single roar of his own.

He snatched a deep breath, but never got to use it.

'With all due respect, *signor*, I think I ought to stay.'

She skidded to a halt, almost within his reach. Her voice had been little more than a whisper. He hadn't expected that. When she glanced nervously at the front of the house before speaking again she surprised him a second time.

'For a little while, at least. Please?'

Totally wrong-footed, Gianni was stunned into silence. Not by what she said, but by the way she said it. An arrow of thought shot through his brain. *It's almost as though she's as concerned for the staff as I am...but, no, she couldn't be...*

Words hissed through his clenched teeth like a November blast.

'You have the nerve to speak to *me* of respect? A woman who bursts in on a house in crisis with laughter?'

Meg was so close she could hear the breath labouring in and out through his parted lips. She was petrified, but desperation kept her standing firm. She had to hope that she could make her new boss see reason and keep her on. It was vital.

'I meant no harm, *signor*. I would never have made such a fuss if I'd known the circumstances. Can't we draw a line under all this and start again?'

Within seconds she realised her mistake. Gianni Bellini had no reverse gear.

From the moment she'd arrived, she had realised this was going to be difficult. Now it looked close to impossible. She felt weak with terror, but couldn't let him see that. She needed this job. Too many people were relying on her to simply roll over and accept what this strangely changed Gianni said.

With nothing to lose but her dignity, Meg pressed on. She lowered her lids. It was a slow, methodical gesture like that of a diver standing on the topmost board. To her surprise, he reacted by giving her time to speak.

'When your father was alive, he specifically wanted me to come and work here,' she said with measured calm. 'I was the most highly qualified applicant for the post, and without my skill his plants will soon suffer. He had all sorts of plans in mind for the Castelfino Estate. Now he's…well, let's just say he'll need a fitting memorial. He was always worrying about the future, and a lot of his ideas were practical. He spoke about throwing open his plant collection to the public one day, as a way of encouraging tourism in the area. I'm sure you'll be carrying on all his other good works, *signor*,' she added, and was relieved to see her in-nocent remark seemed to impress him. 'Any man would be proud to leave such a legacy. Believe me, I know.'

His attitude hardened. 'How do you know? Because you have a fistful of paper qualifications?' he scoffed, clearly unimpressed.

'No, I can say it because my father was exactly the same,' she said evenly. 'When he was taken seriously ill, he spent so much time worrying about what he would leave behind, he couldn't rest. He was his own worst enemy. Your father was a good, kind man, *signor*. He deserves a living tribute. I worked with him closely on his new project here. He was so keen for it to go ahead, I really think it would be a mistake for you to cancel it just yet.'

Gianni stared at her for a long time. Then the corners of his mouth lifted in the slow, devastating smile that had been haunting all her dreams since their first meeting. He took a step forward, and held out his hand. 'Allow me to congratulate you, Miss—?'

'Imsey. Megan Imsey.'

His fingers felt deliciously warm as he enfolded her hand. It was a heat reflected in the colour of her cheeks.

'Well done, Miss Imsey. I'm lost for words—something that has never happened to me before!'

Meg smiled back. She was a fast learner. In the last few minutes Gianni Bellini had morphed from her dream man into a living, breathing human being. Someone she could reach out and touch. To her surprise she realised they had at least two things in common. Work was everything to him—and he was as good at hiding his real feelings as she was. He might have started off as her fantasy lover, but Meg recognised a realist when she met one. Brought up on the breadline by devoted parents, she had become ultra ambitious to try to cushion them from poverty. She needed this job, for their sake. If that wasn't reason enough to make a stand, Gianni Bellini was so magnetic. His playboy side had entranced her at Chelsea. He was so much more glamorous than anyone she had met before. Now he had been catapulted into a position of power, she wanted to see what his ambitions would make of her careful plans.

'Surely you don't need to make a snap decision about something as insignificant to you as my job, *signor*? Right now, you must have a thousand and one other things to think about.'

That at least was uncontroversial. He might be practised in the art of blocking his emotions, but for a split second Meg saw pain in his eyes. Anyone else would have missed it, but she'd been in some cold, dark places herself. She remembered how it had felt when her own father was hovering between life and death. With a pang she put her hand out to her new employer, but couldn't quite manage the intimacy of a touch. Instead she withdrew, and let her words convey her sympathy. 'And top of that list should be *you*.'

Her feelings were totally genuine, but they weren't welcome. Gianni frowned.

'No…I'm all right.'

'You look as though you've been out all night,' Meg said, torn between sympathy and adding the judgemental word *again*. It was hard not to remember all those plants she had gift-wrapped for his string of girlfriends.

'I wasn't there when it happened,' he muttered, almost to himself. 'I was in a nightclub with a thousand other people, none of whom would have cared if I dropped dead in front of them. I went straight to the hospital and sat beside him, trying as hard as I could to feel something. There was nothing…but then—'

He stopped.

'It's OK,' Meg said softly, reaching out again. This time her dreams didn't come into it. She laid her hand lightly on his sleeve, but taking a step backward he quickly put himself out of her reach again.

'Then I came straight back here because this place won't run itself…' Gianni's words began briskly enough but the lids of his olive-dark eyes were growing heavier all the time. He checked his watch. '*Dio!* I haven't been to bed for days…' he finished with weary disbelief.

'I can see that,' Meg said softly. He looked as though he had been sleeping in his beautiful designer clothes. As she watched he put a clenched fist up to his brow and scrubbed at it roughly. Meg knew how he felt. She had fretted for days and nights about her own father, when he was lying in Intensive Care.

Her memories were still too raw, and suddenly they overwhelmed her. Rushing forward, she put her arms out to him. She couldn't help herself. His reaction was equally instinctive as he threw up his hands to stop her.

'No! It's fine. Please—don't.'

Meg stopped. Forced to resist the urge to comfort him, she mirrored his gesture with one of peace.

'All right—all right—you're concerned that we're being watched by your staff. I know. But you aren't doing yourself or anybody else any favours by going beyond the point of exhaustion, *signor.* You need rest, and unless you get some *you'll* be in hospital, too! Who will take care of the Villa Castelfino and all your staff then?'

He looked at her steadily for a long time. As he did so

his dark, enigmatic expression began to stir a transformation deep within her body. Meg reacted to his scrutiny like a bud growing beneath snow. Gianni Bellini was unshaven and exhausted, yet he still looked totally irresistible. All the wicked fantasies she had dared to dream about him filtered back into her mind. She had spent so many long, lonely nights remembering his face, his smile, all his easy charm. Now here he was, right here in front of her. She began to blush. Something that began as heat rising from her breasts to her cheeks blossomed into the colour of a guinée rose, and silenced her.

'Why are you doing this, Megan Imsey? You've only just got here. Why should you care about me? I'm a cold, unfeeling taskmaster. You'll hear that from anyone outside the clubs and beaches. When I shelve all my father's wild ideas, there'll be no job here for you.'

Meg raised her eyebrows. The old count's plans had all seemed perfectly sensible to her. This was her dream job, but there was definitely no place for daydreams in Gianni's new regime. It was time to tell him some of her hard home truths.

'I can't afford *not* to care,' she said in a careful, matter-of-fact voice. If he wouldn't recognise simple compassion, that must mean he didn't want any. 'I'm on the Villa Castelfino payroll, but so far you're the only person here who knows I've turned up for duty. To put it bluntly, it's in my interests to take great care of you if I ever want to be reimbursed for this pointless jaunt, Signor Bellini. And there's always an outside chance you might see reason, and stick with the old count's plans as I suggest,' she finished boldly.

It took some time, but Gianni's expression gradually moved from resignation to distaste. 'I might have guessed. With women, it all comes down to money in the end. And people wonder why I keep them all at arm's length!' He grimaced at last.

His reply was a final wake-up call for Meg. In real life, he was turning out to be quite a different prospect from the ideal man she wanted. With regret, she recognised he was as practical and down-to-earth as she was. It was beginning to feel as though work was the only certainty in her life. With no illusions left about Gianni, all she could hope to do was to secure her future. Apart from all the pressing practical reasons, her parents had waved her off at the airport with such high hopes for her. She couldn't bear to disappoint them by returning home without achieving anything.

'It isn't simply money, *signor*. Common sense and practicality come into it, too. My family back home are relying on me as a backstop. I've put their business back on an even keel. They're doing really well at the moment but we all know from bitter experience how circumstances can change overnight.'

When she said that, Gianni briefly made eye contact with her. He nodded, but didn't speak.

'That's why I need this job, *signor*. Your father arranged for me to live in the Garden Cottage here on the Villa Castelfino estate. I've visited before, so I know where it is. There's no need to worry about me,' she said, in the unlikely event Gianni Bellini ever worried about anyone but himself. 'I can sort myself out. I'll be absolutely no trouble. We can talk about all this later. You just see about getting yourself some rest.'

'No. I need to be alert.'

He looked as belligerent as only a sleep-deprived man could look.

'Of course you do, *signor*.' Meg smiled as he played

straight into her hands. 'That's why you must get some sleep. Don't worry; I've already had some experience of how this house works. They'll keep you informed. You won't miss a thing,' she said soothingly. 'The previous count was always telling me he was careful to employ only the very best staff.'

Gianni locked eyes with her for a long time. Then unexpectedly he took her hand again and raised it to his lips for another heart-stopping kiss. It brought back every spine-tingling sensation he had ever evoked in her, and left her gasping. When he looked at her now his expression overflowed with all the dark promise she remembered from their first meeting.

Then he said slowly, 'Yes. He was. I can see that now.'

CHAPTER TWO

GIANNI followed Meg's instructions only by default. He was so tired his body took complete control of his mind. Leaving the new arrival to fend for herself, he trudged up to his suite. Working entirely on autopilot, he kicked off his shoes and fell into bed.

The next thing he knew, he was waking up with the sun in his eyes and hunger gnawing a hole in his stomach. Grabbing his bedside phone, he rang Housekeeping to order some food. Megan was right, he told himself. He *had* needed sleep. He must have been out of action for hours.

Twenty minutes later, shaved, showered and feeling slightly more human, he walked into the dining room of his suite. A meal was being laid out on its central table. His body clock told him it should be dinner. It didn't look like it. In fact, it didn't look like anything that had appeared on the Villa Castelfino's menu in all his thirty-two years.

'That food looks delicious,' he said suspiciously, picking up the neatly folded copy of *La Repubblica* lying on his tray.

'It is, *signor*. Some of us were invited to lunch over at the Garden Cottage today, and the head gardener gave us this to eat, too.'

Before Gianni could question the man further, he noticed something.

'This is Monday's newspaper. What happened to Sunday, Rodolfo?'

'The indoor staff had strict instructions not to disturb you, *signor*.'

The man put such an odd emphasis on the word 'indoor' that Gianni's mind filled instantly with suspicion. He walked around the table, surveying his unlikely meal from every angle. There were cheese palmiers with half a dozen different sorts of salads and a cut glass dish of something brightly coloured.

'This looks like English trifle. I haven't seen that since I was at school. Where did it come from?'

'The head gardener suggested some amendments to your menu, *signor*.'

Gianni stopped pacing. Frowning, he shook a finger in the air. '*That* was what I was going to ask you a moment ago. I didn't know we *had* a head gardener,' he said slowly, suspecting he already knew what had happened. The girl who had invited herself into his estate had become a cuckoo in the nest the moment he turned his back.

'Miss Imsey has only recently arrived, *signor*.'

'Oh…*her*,' Gianni said with the airy exhaustion of a man who had a million employees, all of them more trouble than they were worth. 'Well, don't worry. She won't be here for long. I'm more interested in practical skills than paper qualifications. People who hide from life by studying are always afraid of hard work.' He was quite confident in his views, but the look on Rodolfo's face instantly made him suspicious again. 'Oh, now *don't* say you've been taken in by that face, or those legs…her smile, that rivulet of hair or those baby blue eyes…'

Gianni's tone began to waver along with his conviction. Straightening his jacket like a prosecuting counsel, he brought himself briskly back to the ancestral line. No member of staff could be allowed to run riot around the place. It didn't matter how pretty and distracting she was.

'Or anything else, for that matter!' He added sharply. 'That girl is only interested in one thing—collecting her wages. She told me so herself, the moment she arrived.'

Gianni's waiter was in no hurry to leave. It was obvious he had something more to say. Reaching for a second cheese palmier, Gianni gave him a stare calculated to squeeze tears from a commando.

'You look like you've got something else to tell me, Rodolfo.'

The man coughed politely. 'You may like to know that Cook is currently wearing a face like an old lemon, *signor*.'

Gianni was bringing the serving tongs from the silver salver to his plate. When he heard those words, he stopped. The thought that Meg had been nice to him only so she could get paid was irritating. News that she could manage to annoy his staid old cook brought a grudging smile back to his face.

'This wouldn't have anything to do with the new head gardener, would it?' he asked innocently.

'*Sì*, Count.'

'And…morale in the kitchens is…?' Gianni probed, brushing pastry crumbs from his fingertips.

'On the way up.'

'I always said the Bellini family lets good staff have its head,' Gianni said in a warm glow of self-satisfaction.

Dismissing the waiter, he settled down to enjoy his meal. He was ravenous, and ate himself to a standstill. It was the first time he could ever remember sitting in the Villa Castelfino and pushing away a plate because he was full, rather than nauseous. It was then he realised he was beginning to feel better than he had done in years. As well as the improved diet, in one day he had managed to get more sleep than he normally did in a week. Then reality kicked in again. His father was dead. The future of hundreds of hectares of real estate and thousands of staff across the globe relied on him, in his capacity as the new Count di Castelfino. His business could expand now, exactly as planned.

Walking over to his sound system, he put on some music. Then he went out onto the balcony leading from his private dining room. From there he could survey the scene at his leisure. All the land below him, right out as far as the sheltering hills, was now his responsibility. Until a few days ago, his vineyard had occupied fewer than a hundred hectares of the vast estate. That was set to change. Gianni had his gaze fixed firmly on the future. His nights of excess were behind him. From now on, improving his wine business would absorb all his waking moments. It saved him having to think about the one aspect of aristocratic life that loomed over him like a cloud of volcanic ash. He didn't want to be the last man to bear his name and title—but neither did he want to see a child suffer by being born into the Bellini family. The taste of that was still bitter in his own mouth.

He sat down to reflect on the view, trying to avoid thinking about the inevitable. It was quite a distraction. He had never really looked at the landscape outside his suite before. It had simply always been there. Now every vine, olive tree and cypress belonged to him. He relaxed in his seat contentedly.

And then Megan Imsey walked into view, pushing a wheelbarrow loaded with tools. A broad brimmed straw hat shaded her expression, but Gianni could see she was enjoying herself in the sunshine. As he watched she turned her head this way and that, looking at the desiccated grasses sprawling over the weedy path. She must be heading for the walled garden, he realised. Work was already well under way there, on his father's last project. It was an extravagance of greenhouses, wild enough to bankrupt the Bellini coffers. His study of her became critical. Why was she going there when he had already told her what he thought of his father's plans? And what sort of person worked when they didn't have to, in any case?

With that, Gianni's scorn slipped into a smile. He only had to think of the times he'd rolled home at first light, still on a champagne-fuelled high. He'd stopped off at his vineyard many times, to work off his excess energy. An attitude like that had carved him a spectacular career as a wine producer in only a few years. He had done it by applying the same guidelines he used in his private life— if you want something done properly, do it yourself.

He wondered if Miss Megan Imsey had a similar interest in quality control. This might be the perfect moment to find out. It was a beautiful day, and he was feeling lucky...

The Tuscan sun clung to Meg like a second skin. To call it hot was an understatement. Beneath her long sleeved white shirt, baggy overalls, shady straw hat and sunglasses she was coated in sunscreen. It might be safe, but it felt totally suffocating. Despite the heat she bowled along through the gardens at a good pace. She was always eager to get to work, but the Villa Castelfino had one big novelty that made it really special. A hundred years ago, an earlier count had built his aristocratic young English wife a walled kitchen garden to stop her feeling homesick. Nothing had been done with it for years, until Gianni's father had hatched this scheme for a grand range of state-of-the-art greenhouses. The new complex was almost finished, but on this sunny morning Meg was more interested in the undeveloped parts of the garden. Its faded melancholy really appealed to her. Smiling, she unlocked the garden door and let herself into one whole hectare of heaven.

She stood for a moment and relished her achievement. This was what she had spent the last few months planning and supervising on her trips to Italy. A glass palace took centre stage in the secret garden. There were still a few cosmetic touches to add, but the main building was pretty much complete. This morning the entire roof was open to catch every available breeze. It looked like a stately galleon in full sail. Flushed with success, Meg wondered how Gianni could possibly dislike such a lovely thing. With a pang of fear, she wondered how she could persuade him to keep her on. She couldn't bear to think of anyone tampering with her beautiful greenhouses. This success had given her a welcome boost, on top of saving her parents' business from bankruptcy. The possibility they might slip back while she was away was enough to worry about. Her fragile self-confidence didn't need this project to founder as well.

To cheer herself up, Meg turned her attention to the rest

of the garden. Once upon a time it had produced all the food for the villa. Decades of neglect meant it was now nothing more than an area of infrequently mown grass and overgrown fruit trees. Without regular care their long, lissom branches grew in all directions, throwing welcome pools of shade throughout the day. She parked her barrow in one of these slightly cooler spots, beside an ancient dipping pool. Then she went back and locked the garden door. That would ensure she wasn't disturbed. Returning to her barrow full of tools and provisions, she tied one end of a length of twine around the neck of her water bottle. Lowering it into the dipping pool would keep the contents chilled. Then she started work.

The structural work of repairing the hard landscaping was complete, so it was left to Meg to begin the best job of all. She was about to mark out new flowerbeds, and couldn't wait to get started. There would be borders at the foot of the encircling wall, designed to complement the new garden buildings. Meg's mind had been turning over ideas for a long time. Now she needed to see them marked out on the ground, to get a feel for how they might work in reality. Once she had the details right, work could start. That meant there would be something worth seeing by the end of the week. The bigger the impact she could make on Gianni Bellini, the more likely he was to let her stay. Or so she hoped.

She began measuring up and marking out, but soon felt overdressed. The first things to go were her sandals. The short, prickly grass beneath her bare feet made her laugh with the excitement of it all. She was making the closest possible contact with this grand estate, and it was fun! Curling her toes into the hot turf she carried on, hammer-

ing in pegs and laying out string to plan the new flowerbeds. There was so little air movement that soon her hat
and shirt began to cling uncomfortably in the heat. She
hesitated for a moment, wondering if she was brave enough
to strip off completely. Glancing around, she came to a
decision. The garden wasn't overlooked. Working in her
underwear was no worse than wearing a bikini, and she had
worked in one of those often enough at home. The door into
her sanctuary was locked. No one would see. If she was
careful to avoid getting sunburned, no one would ever
know.

Impulsively, she tore off her outer clothes and went
back to work. When the sun parched her skin too fiercely,
she dodged back into the shade and enjoyed a drink of
pool-cooled water from her bottle. She was straightening
up to assess how the outline was developing when a frighteningly familiar voice almost sent her into orbit.

'Is this how all English gardeners dress, Megan?'

Meg whirled around and her heart stood still. It was
Gianni: the *real* one, not the exhausted version who had
tried to send her away the day before. Today he looked
every inch as seductive as he had done at the Chelsea
Flower Show. That alarmed her as much as his anger had
done.

'What are you doing here?' she burst out, her hands
trying ineffectually to cover all the bits her scanty underwear was failing to hide.

He nodded towards the villa. 'I live here, remember?'

Meg was caught completely off guard. 'I'm sorry—
how could I possibly forget?' She gasped. A blush was no
defence against him. He continued looking at her with undisguised interest.

'You certainly seemed to have done.'

'I never dreamed anyone would disturb me in here. The door was locked. I have the only key. How did you get in?' she blustered, embarrassment mixed up with growing anger.

One hand in his pocket, Gianni strolled over to the old medlar tree where Meg had hung her hat and shirt. Plucking them from the branches like particularly desirable fruit, he made his way over to her. He took his time. It was painfully obvious to Meg that he was making her wait for her clothes. She wasn't in the mood to be toyed with. As soon as he got close enough she snatched her things from his hands and pulled them on. He watched with something close to amusement. Then he drew a second key from his pocket with a flourish.

'As I said—I live here. I have a copy of every key in the place.'

Barefoot but otherwise decent, Meg rallied.

'That doesn't explain why you felt the need to come in here.'

'It wasn't a need. It was a want. I wanted to see you, Megan.'

There was a haunting look in his dark eyes. It was so delicious she could hardly meet his gaze. Nervous that he might be able to read all sorts of things from her own expression, she looked down at the coarse wiry grass at her feet. All sorts of hope were beginning to stir deep within her, but there was only one she could put into words.

'I hope you're feeling better, Count.'

His smile widened, bright as pearl against the golden warmth of his skin. 'Yes, I am—but call me Gianni, please.'

Meg's heart did a little skip—until she realised he probably gave that bonus to all his staff.

'Part of the reason I came out here was to thank you,' he went on. 'You were right. I was overtired when you arrived. All I've done since then is sleep—and enjoy an excellent late lunch.'

'That's good,' Meg said with genuine relief.

'Afterwards I went down to the kitchens, where they told me that the meal I so enjoyed was your idea. What made you challenge Cook?'

She looked up quickly to find out exactly how much trouble she was in. In response Gianni smiled, raising his eyebrows in silent approval. It was an expression that made her shiver, despite the heat.

'You looked so distracted. I knew eating would be way down on your list of priorities. When I saw steak on today's menu I thought it sounded far too heavy for this weather. I decided to cater for myself, and guessed you might like something light and familiar too. I'd already discovered from chatting with the other staff that you attended boarding school in England. It just so happens my aunt is now Head Chef at the same place. I rang and asked her what dishes would be most popular at your old school on a day like today.'

Meg didn't add that everyone loved comfort food in times of trouble, but could see he knew that already. The softening around his eyes proved it to her.

'That shows real initiative, Megan,' he said with conviction. 'Especially in view of what happened when you suggested it to my cook. I've come straight from the kitchens. As soon as she has finished the larder inventory, she'll be coming out to apologise to you for the things she said.'

Meg blinked at him. An apology was the very last thing she expected, in the circumstances.

'Pardon?'

'The staff said she tried to pull rank, but you stood your ground. Well done. You're the first member of staff who's done that to her.'

'Are you saying you don't mind?' Meg said warily. People grand enough to employ gardeners never usually bothered to praise their staff.

'I'm delighted, Megan.' His voice lilted slowly over her name, trying it out for size.

'Are you *sure* you don't mind?' She asked uncertainly. 'I mean, I hadn't been here for more than two minutes before picking a blazing row with your cook. She's an old family faithful; I'm the new arrival—and you're taking *my* side?'

Gianni searched her face, mystified that she seemed incapable of taking in what he had said. 'But of course. It's the only stance to take. She was wrong, you were right. One of my first duties as the new count was going to be to go through all the menus. You got there before me, that's all.' He saw her face flush deeply. Instantly concerned, he reached out to her. His strong brown hands grasped her elbows to give support. 'Megan? What's the matter? It must be the sun. Here—I'll help you to a seat.'

She looked down at his fingers. They slid over her skin and closed around her with exactly the same relish she had conjured up in all her fantasies. It was wonderful.

'There's no need…I'm fine.' She gasped, barely able to raise her voice above a whisper. The sheer delight of feeling his touch was breathtaking. 'I've just had a bit of a surprise, that's all. I—I thought the only men who weren't afraid of cooks were head gardeners,' she improvised quickly.

Gianni let go of her, offended. '*I* make the rules here.

All of them. And that includes whether or not we employ a female head gardener,' he finished with slow, devastating meaning.

Meg was alert immediately. 'What do you mean?'

She bounced the question straight at him, but could see he wasn't fooled for a minute. Gianni wouldn't be taking any chances with her. Anyone who could put a cook on the back foot as she had done would need to be watched carefully.

He looked down at her for a few seconds longer than was strictly necessary before giving her a meaningful shrug.

'That rather depends.'

'Thank goodness for that, as my original title was Curator of Exotic Plants. I'm no Head Gardener—though I'm more than qualified to do it,' she added quickly, 'But when I saw how things were here, I knew the staff wouldn't take kindly to a newcomer's suggestions so I took a chance and borrowed the title for a minute. The whole kitchen staff fell for it.' She finished with a nervous little laugh.

To her amazement Gianni's devastating smile burst into life, but he was careful to quash it almost straight away.

'That's what I call insight. A girl who shows insight *and* initiative? You'll go far, *ragazza insolente*!'

Tiny muscles quivered all around his lips. Meg could see he was trying not to laugh. What made it worse was that he knew *she* knew. It wasn't the sort of position she wanted to put her new boss in. Especially when that boss was Gianni Bellini, a man guaranteed to have any girl he wanted.

Dutifully, she looked down at the grass again to hide her own smile, but wasn't about to stifle her ambition.

'I already have, *signor*,' she said, careful to hide any hint of humour. 'I graduated top of my intake, I saved my parents' business from ruin, then I landed the top job here. And I haven't finished yet.'

'I'm beginning to realise that,' he said quietly. 'So, Miss Curator of Exotic Plants—what are your plans for my new garden?'

Meg sensed he was trying to lighten the tone. Despite the twinkle in his eyes, she decided to tread carefully until she was certain where she stood with him.

'I'm here to implement the old count's plans, not my own,' she said carefully. 'At the moment, his collection of tropical plants is restricted to that old lemon house at the far end of the kitchen garden. They were all going to be moved and the collection expanded into this new glass-house range as soon as it was finished.'

She began walking off toward a long, low building set against a distant wall. Gianni did not follow her immediately. When he did, he lingered a few steps behind.

'Am I walking too fast for you, Gianni?'

'Not at all,' he said airily. 'It's a beautiful day, and I have a beautiful view. Why hurry?'

She looked back over her shoulder and realised what he was watching.

'*Signor!*'

'I've told you before—my name is Gianni.'

'Not when you're looking at my bottom like that, it isn't,' Meg said, desperately reminding herself how many plants he had bought from her stand at the Chelsea Flower Show. He had done it to keep all the women in his life happy. She had no intention of becoming one among many. Even though her limbs turned to water whenever he looked at her in that deep, meaningful way...

The original lemon house had been built with an open front. Later on, its graceful stone arches had been glazed to create a greenhouse. Meg opened the door on its riot of damp, lush leaves and exotic flowers.

'Isn't this wonderful?' She took in a leisurely lungful of the warm, moist air. It was rich with the fragrance of bark and tropical flowers.

'As a twenty-first century woman, I hope you're being ironic,' Gianni observed drily, following her into the building. 'Keeping these plants in luxury must cost the earth, both in money and resources. Air conditioning isn't in vogue, Megan—especially for flowers,' he finished severely.

'Oh, I know it's extravagant and old fashioned.' Meg ran her hand lovingly over one of the crumbling stone pillars. 'That's why the count wanted me to build him a dedicated range of greenhouses, to give his plants ideal growing conditions. That means computer-controlled atmospheres. He wanted to include the latest equipment and ideas, so that everything will be perfect. He intended his estate to be a showcase. His idea was that this part of the Val di Castelfino should become an extra special tourist attraction, and an example of best practice.'

'How does this steam-filled white elephant qualify?' Gianni was haughty. 'Had my father never heard of climate change? I'm surprised someone as well qualified as you didn't put him right, Megan. My father always lived in the past. An educated woman like you must be well briefed in all the drawbacks.'

Meg knew it wasn't her place to comment, but a point of honour was at stake. She tried to pin a bold stare on him, but it was difficult when he could out-stare her so easily. 'You don't seem impressed by my qualifications, *signor*.'

Though outwardly calm, she was trembling too much to say any more. His penetrating gaze made her too light headed for words. Instead she raised her eyebrows, simply inviting more comment.

'In my experience, the more exam success someone has, the less likely they are to get their hands dirty. I'd rather someone had worked their way to the top of the tree, in the same way I've done.'

'With no help from your family name, your position in life or your father?'

There was an ironic lilt in Meg's voice. She regretted it instantly, but Gianni hardly seemed to notice.

'Exactly!' He dropped one hand onto the greenhouse staging with a resounding thump. 'The Castelfino vineyard is my baby, from conception right through to international prize-winning status. I've earned every penny—there's no job on the land I'm not happy to do myself, and I've never had a cent from my father. As you must know,' he finished gruffly.

'I never discussed you with the late count, Gianni. I had no idea you were related to him until a few hours ago, remember.'

His eyes narrowed into channels of suspicion. 'You mean to say he never complained to you about the way I only wanted money spent on cost-effective projects, not his hobbies? I've been studying the work you did for him. All of it—and that includes the dummy sets of figures forwarded to my accountants. Do you deny that they were prepared to stop me discovering exactly how much money my father was frittering away on this…this…?' Exasperated, he waved his hand towards the exotic display of orchids and coloured foliage.

'It was all perfectly legal. The late count's own financial advisors always submitted the correct figures for audit. It was thought you would object to his budget, so he had a separate set made up in case you wanted to inspect them. We didn't want to worry you, that's all.' Meg threw up her head to challenge him with a glare, but something happened. Their eyes met, and for Meg it was the point of no return. She had always thought Gianni was stunning. Now, with the sun lighting a bronze shimmer in his devastating eyes, words didn't do him justice. The breath caught in her throat, stifling all sound. He knew only too well what power lay behind his eyes. As she watched he lowered his lids a fraction, tempting an unconscious sound to escape from her all too self-conscious lips.

'I hope my father didn't lead you to believe that I'm mean.' Gianni's voice was a drawl, as lazy as the air moving through the lemon house. 'On the contrary: I can be the most generous of men if the circumstances—and the woman—are right,' he said, leaving the suggestion in his final words hanging in the air.

'I know. When you were in London I supplied you with all those flowers for your girlfriends, remember?' Meg breathed, trying to keep her voice steady. She was getting dizzy, but it wasn't only the lack of oxygen. The nearness of Gianni in this small, sun-soaked space sent her senses reeling. The light citrus fragrance of his aftershave was so clean and fresh in an atmosphere charged with the heavy hints of bark and mosses. It sent a charge of electricity fizzing down her spine. Without realising it she moved slightly towards him, hungry for contact.

'Then you'll know what I'm going to say next?'

Meg's lips moved, but no sound came out. She knew

what she wanted to hear, but moved her head slowly from side to side.

'I've decided this new range of greenhouses would be a great memorial to my father, after all. You were right to suggest it—very clever, and very provocative. There aren't many women who would think of pampering mere greenery like this.' His voice was as low and inviting as a cool river in the enveloping heat of the tropical house. Meg sighed as his expression softened. The greenhouse she already thought of as hers was working its magic. It was beautiful, and she could make it even better. He could sense that, and she was spellbound.

He was gazing at the wonderful display of brightly coloured flowers and trailing foliage around them, but at any second he might turn that wonderful look on her…at least, that was her dream.

'You're going to cost me a fortune,' he murmured, when she could hardly breathe for suspense.

'That depends on what you want. This is Tuscany. Everything's ripe for enchantment.' Her voice was husky.

'And it all has its price.' He watched her carefully, gauging the effect of his words.

Meg suppressed another sigh. 'Do you agonise like this over your women?' she asked, giving him a knowing look.

'I'm not agonising. It's merely an observation. The price of this new construction is a minor consideration to me. Women are a far more serious matter. There's a lot more than mere money at stake when it comes to the future of my family. The Bellinis haven't lasted this long without being able to pick winners. That's why my father never re-married after my mother died, thank goodness.'

Meg said nothing. The way she fidgeted uncomfortably

within her clothes said it all. She was becoming unbearably hot, but her rising temperature had nothing to do with the tropical house.

'It may sound a harsh judgement to you, Megan, but I know what I'm talking about. When it came to matters of the heart, my father knew his judgement couldn't be trusted.' Gianni continued to gaze at the soft sea of butterfly-bright foliage surrounding them. A playful breeze blew in through the open greenhouse door. It ruffled his dark curls over his brow, giving him a dangerously piratical look. Meg laughed, a little nervously.

'Your father certainly got one thing right,' she said quietly. 'He would be proud of you, Gianni.'

He turned to face her slowly. When Meg got the full benefit of his dark, restless eyes she felt her heart respond. From that moment on she knew that if he ever made a move on her she would be powerless to resist. It was a perfect dream, but something she couldn't dare risk in reality. This job meant a lot to her, and her family. She wasn't about to throw it away for a boss's whim. Even if that boss was gorgeous Gianni...

'I hope he would be proud of me. That's exactly what I intend. I gave him a lot of grief when he was alive, Megan. The least I can do is respect his wishes now. Let's hope I never have to make a choice between my heart and my heritage.' His brow creased as though with the effort of fighting some inner demon.

'Why should you?' Meg asked innocently, not knowing what she was letting herself in for.

'Any number of local "princesses" are desperate to become my wife,' he sighed. 'The Bellini family blueprint says I should choose one of them. She should be installed in one of my town houses as my official partner and mother of my heir. There she'll enjoy a life of pleasure. But that way of life went out with the Middle Ages! Life has moved on. It's all so different now. Marriage isn't simply a matter of duty and honour. It's all pre-nups and making watertight arrangements to secure every stick and stone of my assets for the inevitable divorce.'

To hear him talk about marriage as nothing more than another agreement to be crossed off his list of 'things to do' disappointed Meg.

'There shouldn't be anything inevitable about divorce! No one should marry for anything less than love,' she said firmly, stroking her fingers down the long, leathery leaf of a miltonia. Meg was the last person to contradict an employer, but some things ought to be set in stone. 'Women usually have their own careers nowadays. Marriage isn't seen as the only life for them. And they aren't all grasping parasites.'

'I love women. Don't get me wrong,' Gianni said quickly. 'It's just that the Italian thoroughbred model holds no interest for me.'

'Then you'll have to find someone else.'

'There *is* no one else. All the women I meet are out for everything they can get—believe me.'

Meg was busy adjusting the ties securing a budding flower stem and replied without thinking. 'I'm not.'

Gianni sighed. 'That's what you say now. But I wonder…'

His voice was heavy with regret. It was such a heartfelt comment that she looked up sharply. In that instant all trace of a smile vanished from his face. He was deadly serious—and all Meg's wildest, most wanton fantasies were reflected in his eyes.

She caught her breath. She could not look away—and didn't want to.

And then suddenly she was in his arms.

CHAPTER THREE

THEY kissed with a passion that was totally consuming. His hands held her close to his body. Her fingers tangled in his hair, desperate for him. It was everything she had ever dreamed about, all she wanted and would ever need, and more than was right. But…this was wrong in so many ways. Pitched through passion on a tidal surge of excitement, Meg took precious seconds to catch her breath and call a halt.

'No! Gianni, stop!'

Alarmed, he let her go. 'What's the matter?'

'Nothing…not now…'

'That's all right, then!' His hold on her tightened and he chuckled with a sound as irresistible as chocolate.

'No!' she yelled, all her conviction boiling up again. 'Don't you have *any* morals?'

'Not when it comes to a girl as beautiful as you…' He dropped his face to her hair and began nuzzling it playfully.

Meg had to act fast, and totally against instinct. Her fantasies had primed her to find him irresistible. Now she was actually feeling his touch for herself, she was almost at the point of no return. Fighting against the urge to melt into his coiling embrace, she braced her hands against his shoulders and levered herself out of his grasp.

'Oh, no, how could I forget? Of course you don't have any morals!' she retorted, trying to shock him into retreat. 'After all, you're Gianni Bellini, international ladies' man, aren't you?'

Gianni wasn't shocked by anything, especially a girl barely half his size. He was flushed and breathing fast but did not release her straight away. Despite that, Meg sensed she was out of danger. The smile returned to his face. His irresistible charm should have made him more dangerous, not less, but in a strange way she realised he was no longer a threat to her—for the moment at least. She already knew Gianni Bellini had a highly developed sense of family loyalty. He wasn't the sort of man to risk a scandal by forcing himself on an unwilling member of staff—especially a new member of the team. They were likely to run straight to the press.

'I came here to work at the Villa Castelfino, not to become a source of entertainment for you,' she said firmly, in case he was still in any doubt.

Gianni said nothing, but let his hands slide reluctantly away from her body. She looked down to see him bury them deeply in his pockets.

'I'll take that as your agreement, Gianni.'

He paused before replying. 'Think of it more as a qualified acceptance, binding on neither side,' he said with a flash of roguish humour.

The nerve of the man took her breath away.

'There really is no arguing with you, is there?'

'No. As you will soon discover from the rest of my staff, Megan, when it comes to work, it's my way or the highway. I wanted to find out exactly how keen you are to keep this job.'

Despite the lightness of his tone, Meg detected a sinister meaning behind his words. From feeling flushed and excited, she went hot and cold with dread.

'Does that mean…you're going to sack me after what's just happened?'

Gianni looked genuinely shocked. 'Of course not! That would be illegal. But, *far* more importantly as far as I'm concerned, it would be immoral. This is the twenty-first century. I may be your employer, but that doesn't mean I can force myself on you, against your will. What *do* you think I am?'

Meg's eyes opened wider than she thought physically possible. Gianni looked as innocent as a priest as he stood in front of her, his hands now outstretched in a gesture of disbelief. Yet only a moment ago he had treated her to a ten-second burst of absolute temptation.

When she didn't answer, he clicked his tongue in exasperation. Then he reached out and touched a wayward lock of her hair gently back from her forehead.

'I'm interested in having a good time, but pleasing women is a big part of my enjoyment, Megan.' His fingers trailed from her brow, lingering around the smooth curve of her cheek before falling away with obvious regret. 'Blackmail and bullying have no place in my life. If you're not scared off by what just happened, but you don't want to sleep with me, then that's fine. It's your problem, not mine. '

He gave her a crooked smile of rueful acceptance. Meg was lost all over again. She desperately wanted to throw herself back into his arms, but found she couldn't move. The look in his eyes riveted her to the spot. Then he spoke again, and burst her bubble of temptation.

'Originally, I came out here to warn you that Cook will be arriving in peace. She won't expect you to declare Round Two, so be careful not to take your sexual frustration out on her, won't you?'

With that, he strolled away.

As Meg watched him walk nonchalantly along the greenhouse path a terrifying truth surged through her body. She *did* want to sleep with Gianni Bellini.

She wanted it more than anything she had ever wanted in her entire life.

From that moment on, Meg's excitement at working in a totally alien environment took a back seat. Thoughts of Gianni Bellini coloured her days and haunted her nights. He had totally bewitched her at their first meeting. As a fantasy lover he was ideal. With those devastating looks and charm, he had no drawbacks. The spell he held over her refused to be broken. Despite her dream becoming reality, his power over her increased rather than dimmed. Although their paths rarely crossed, from that moment on Meg was in heaven. All she dreamed about was their torrid kiss, but as far as Gianni was concerned it might never have happened. He showed no signs of wanting to repeat their wonderful experience. He spent most of each day shut away in the Castelfino estate office. Meg spent virtually all her time out in the gardens and grounds. That meant her chances of catching sight of him were remote. That didn't stop her keeping a keen lookout for him. His words circled her mind in a torrent of temptation. '...*pleasing women is a big part of my enjoyment...*' Her mind continually played with everything that might mean. Gianni had accused her of being sexually frustrated. If she was, it was because of him. With only one long-term relationship in her life, Meg was no expert when it came to romance. She used study to save her having to mix with people. Until her first meeting with Gianni, Meg hadn't realised how much she was missing. He had set light to the fuse of her desire. Now everything about him made her desperate to find out more.

Gavin, her only serious boyfriend, had been too heavy-handed. He was fine as a friend, but he had kept trying to push Meg further than she had wanted to go. On top of that, he had tried to monopolise every second of her free time while she had wanted to study. Meg had resented that. After watching her parents struggle to pick things up by experience, she knew the value of gaining proper qualifications. She was in no hurry to curtail her career by making a serious romantic commitment, either. Or so she had always thought in the past...

Gianni Bellini had come into her life and thrown all her careful plans into chaos. He was like no other man she had met before. Always in her thoughts, he wasn't often in her sight. Once or twice she saw him pacing around the cypress walk, deep in conversation on his mobile phone. While he was totally absorbed like that, she watched him. It was wonderful. She indulged herself, gazing at him for seconds on end. That was so much more satisfying than the quick glimpses she got when he strode out to inspect the estate with one of his tenants or managers.

Evenings presented Meg with some of her greatest pleasures, and her worst tortures. Her new home stood not far from the villa's driveway. She always knew when Gianni was going out for the evening. His frighteningly fast Ferrari was just getting into its stride as it accelerated past Garden Cottage. The first time she heard it, the unexpected roar made her drop a plate of freshly baked cookies. The sudden noise was more terrifying than the RAF's low-flying exercises at home in England. She soon got used to it, but it was a different matter whenever Gianni returned in the not-so-early hours of the morning. There was never any chance of getting back to sleep after being woken like that at three a.m. Guiltily, she would slide out of bed and creep to her window. Then she hid in the shadows, hoping for a glimpse of him. There was always a tiny window of opportunity, between the moments when he sprang from his car, leapt up the front steps and dived into the main house. Each night Meg held her breath, fearing the worst. Gianni had the villa to himself, so she expected him to bring a whole harem back home, every night. It never happened. He always returned alone.

Meg would have been relieved, if it hadn't been for one disturbing fact. Gianni always looked up at her bedroom window before he disappeared into the villa. She was careful to stand well back, and tried everything to avoid being seen. It was no good. His last gesture was always a quick glance at her house. It seemed to be directed straight at her. Meg was mystified. Something must alert him, yet he never confronted her about spying on him. That was stranger still. She knew enough about him by now to sense he wouldn't keep a concern like that bottled up. He would have sought her out at work and said something. It didn't happen. Meg suffered in silence, but it was no hardship compared to the alternative. That would be to give up her nightly vigils, which she would never—*could* never—do.

Lying in bed listening to Gianni's footsteps would be no substitute for watching the living, breathing reality of her fantasy man.

* * *

Meg lived on in an agony of suspense for several more days. She supervised the last adjustments to the magnificent range of greenhouses she had designed without any more visits from Gianni. It was only when she was putting the finishing touches to the planting plan inside the greenhouse that the axe fell. Her mobile phone interrupted her while she was wiring some young orchid plants to an artistic arrangement of tree branches in the new tropical section.

'Miss Imsey? The Count di Castelfino wants to see you in his office.' It was one of Gianni's personal assistants. Meg's heart bounced like a ball at the request.

'OK—when?'

There was a shocked silence. Meg realised this must be the first time anyone had ever tried to keep Gianni Bellini waiting. The reply was terse, and to the point.

'*Immediatamente*, if not sooner!'

Meg didn't need any more of a warning. She ran to obey. Covering the distance between the old kitchen garden and the villa at top speed, she was still brushing chipped bark from the knees of her jeans as she dashed into the estate office. Its noisy hubbub fell silent in an instant. The eyes of every secretary and PA followed the journey of each small brown fleck of bark raining down from Meg's clothes and boots. One woman, as beautiful as a bird of paradise, moved swiftly to sweep up all the bits with a dustpan and brush. A second secretary stepped forward holding a roll of perforated plastic. Chivvying Meg toward an impressive mahogany door labelled 'Strictly No Admittance', she knocked on it loudly.

'Come in!'

Meg had thought she was nervous. Hearing the rich,

smooth sound of Gianni's voice added an extra frisson to her fear. She froze.

How the secretary threw open the door and bowled the roll of perforated plastic inside so casually, Meg had no idea. It uncoiled as an eighteen-inch-wide strip, protecting the highly polished wood floor of Gianni's office.

Meg was desperate to break the tension of her ordeal. 'No red carpet for me, then?' She giggled nervously to the secretary.

'No, only a carpet protector,' the woman snapped, shooing her along.

Meg walked forward. Gianni was sitting behind a vast workstation at the far side of the room. With his back to the windows, head down and engrossed in his work, he presented an imposing figure. Meg wasn't sure what to do. She looked back the way she had come. As she did so the door slammed shut. That cut off any hope of escape. Edging forward, she stopped a respectful distance before the end of the silver plastic road. There she knotted her hands together in an agony of guilt, and waited. It felt as though one end of her nerves were nailed to the tip of Gianni's fountain pen. The further across the page his hand moved, the further they stretched.

He was writing an extremely long sentence.

Outside, swifts screamed across the sky. Dust motes spiralled up the shafts of sunlight thrown across the glassy floor of his office. The heat increased. Meg's temperature rose. Outside, a dog barked down in the village. A clock ticked. The dog barked a second time. Beneath his desk, Gianni shuffled his feet.

He was testing Meg's nerves beyond endurance. Suddenly, she couldn't stand it any more.

'I'm sorry I've been spying on you out of my window at night but it's just that your car always wakes me up when you drive past and I can never get back to sleep after that and it's become a sort of habit that I have to get up and look out to make sure everything's all right and you always happen to look up at the wrong time and—'

Her first word stopped his pen. The rest of them lifted both it, and his head. By the time her voice trickled into silence he was staring at her with naked curiosity.

'That's interesting, Megan. That's *extremely* interesting,' he murmured at last, with a drawl that made her squirm. Throwing his pen down on the blotter, he sat back in his chair. Then he put the tips of his fingers together and looked at her keenly over the top of them.

'Do you know, I had absolutely *no* idea you were doing that, Megan?'

She squirmed some more.

'I actually called you in to my office for a completely different reason. I wanted to find out how you're settling in—nothing more exciting than that. Perhaps you would like to go out, come back in and we'll start this interview all over again?'

She threw another hunted look over her shoulder at the door. It was the only thing standing between her and the complete destruction of her self-esteem.

'Do I have to?'

He gave a low, throaty chuckle. It was calculated to snatch her attention straight back to him, and worked like a charm.

'I wasn't being entirely serious.' His expression had all the delicious amusement she had enjoyed at the Chelsea Flower Show. It had the same effect, too, soothing her nerves just enough to let a little smile escape.

'You might be on to something, Gianni. Running the gauntlet of your beautiful office staff without having had time to take a shower, change my clothes and put on a bit of make-up was a real challenge!'

'There's nothing wrong with the way you look.' His eyes roamed over her body, giving weight to his words.

'They seemed to think so,' she said nervously. 'That's why they rolled this out for me.' She pointed at the carpet protector. Once again he chuckled.

'Don't take it personally. It's done for every visit from a member of my outdoor staff. As well as my own vineyard, I've inherited olive and citrus plantations and any number of farms. A lot of it would end up in here, scattered all over my office floor if they didn't take precautions like that.'

'Your indoor staff aren't like the people who work in the grounds,' Meg said, still stinging from the scornful looks she had been given.

'My domestic staff are all fine, but it's a jungle out there.' He nodded towards the outer room before adding quickly, 'But don't worry—you're of absolutely no interest to my office staff. They don't see *you* as any sort of threat at all.'

Meg wasn't remotely reassured.

'Is that supposed to cheer me up?' she asked faintly.

'Of course. Now—to business. How are you getting on here, Megan? I've been meaning to check up on you for the past few days, but no sooner do I spot you in the garden than you vanish. That's why I've called you in here. I want to talk to you properly.'

'And I wanted to do the same, Gianni,' Meg said before she could stop herself. He was interested straight away.

'That sounds promising. Take a seat.' He indicated a

deeply buttoned visitor's chair drawn up before his workstation.

To reach it she would have to step off the carpet protector. He saw her glance from one to the other and back
again, and laughed.

'Don't bother about the floor. I never normally give my
cleaning staff anything to do. Your little footprints won't
kill them.'

She walked over and sat down in the chair. Elbows on
his desk, Gianni leaned forward, his grin growing predatory. After all her fantasies, all the hours spent wondering
what to say and how to act the next time they met, Meg
froze again. Her wild confession might turn out to have
been a fatal mistake. If he tried anything now, she could
put up no resistance. Trembling, she waited for his next
move. Forcing herself to sit back in her chair, she looked
down at her hands. They were twisting nervously in her lap.

'While I've got the opportunity, Gianni, I'd like to ask
if you could possibly—that is, if you don't mind—if
there's some way…if perhaps you could be a bit quieter
when you return from your nights out?' She finished in a
rush, crimson with embarrassment. Cringing at the way
she had told Gianni everything about her night-time vigils,
she waited for him to laugh.

All she heard was the sound of him sitting back in his
chair. There was an agonisingly long pause. And then he
said distantly, 'I've been thinking about that since the moment you mentioned it. You're the first person to say I've
woken them up. Nobody else has ever complained.'

Meg tried to make a joke of it. 'Perhaps they're afraid
of you!'

'And you aren't?' He sounded curious, rather than cross.

Meg risked glancing up. He looked calm enough, and his beautiful eyes were dark with questions.

'I-I'll have to think about that,' Meg said eventually. It was true. Gianni Bellini could be terrifying. He could also be warm and funny, but Meg wasn't sure how deep or genuine any of his emotions were.

'Don't take too long making up your mind, will you?'

She heard the laughter in his voice and couldn't resist looking up again. Gianni smiled at her over his clasped hands.

'So I've been costing you your beauty sleep, have I? If it's any consolation, it's impossible to tell. Nobody would ever know. Have you thought that, while you're watching me, you could be in bed, getting more rest?'

'There's no point at that time in the morning. I don't bother. I might as well get up, do some paperwork and then go out to work.'

'I know,' he said, quite unrepentant. 'By the time I'm stripped and ready for bed, you're out and about, heading for the gardens.'

She frowned at him quizzically. 'How do you know that?'

All he did was smile as he waited for Meg to work out what he meant. It didn't take long. The footpath from her cottage to the old kitchen gardens passed straight along one side of the villa. His suite must overlook her route. Meg had a sudden, delicious vision of him standing stark naked on the balcony of his bedroom, watching her. At any time over the past days she might have glanced up and caught sight of him in all his glory. But she hadn't. Her shift from puzzlement to disappointment must have been obvious. Gianni responded with a slow, teasing smile that filled her mind with all sorts of possibilities.

'Don't worry. Now I am Count, I shall be partying less and entertaining here at the villa a lot more. You won't be troubled by me during the night too often in the future,' he said with sly humour, as though he knew she always would be. 'I'll be too busy working—and your job is another reason I've asked you here. Something you said on the day you arrived stuck in my mind. I got my staff to check you out, Miss Megan Imsey. Did you ever tell my father you were so grand and so well qualified you turned down a job with the English royal family?'

'No! I'd never say a thing like that, even if it was true!' Meg flapped her hands in embarrassment. 'I didn't turn them down—I couldn't take the job. There's a difference. My father had his heart attack the day after I was offered the position. I'd already accepted, but couldn't take it up. My parents needed me, and all the help I could give them. I knew there would always be another job beyond the palace gardens, but my mum and dad are the only family I've got. People are more important than careers.'

He ignored her. 'I've decided you're wasted here, Megan.' The breath caught in her throat. What could he mean?

'That title, Curator of Exotic Plants, confines you in those glass prisons behind the ten-foot-high walls of my kitchen garden. I want to set you free, Megan. You're going to take on the role of my Head Gardener, here at the Villa Castelfino. If you live up to my very high expectations, there could well be a promotion to Co-ordinator of Horticulture for all my properties—Barbados, Diamond Isle, Manhattan, and the rest.'

Meg could hardly take it in. Gianni was speaking so casually, and yet the job he was talking about would mean the world to her.

He stood up and pushed back his chair. Strolling around his desk, he perched on the corner, one leg swinging. The toe of his handmade leather shoe was only inches from her knee. Looking down on her from his vantage point, he tried to reassure her. It had exactly the opposite effect.

'There will, of course, be all sorts of fringe benefits.' His beautiful face was slowly lit by a meaningful smile.

Meg gazed up at him. Her future career lay in the hands of this bewitching, desirable man. From the look in those haunting dark eyes, she was only a heartbeat away from a still more torrid destiny.

'First on the list is a dress allowance,' he announced.

Meg looked down at what she was wearing. Her simple white T-shirt showed off her new tan beautifully, but neither it nor her jeans were new. On the other hand, they were comfortable.

'But these clothes are best for my job,' she murmured.

Gianni grimaced. 'They may be in England, but here you are part of my new Villa Castelfino Project. I have decided my vineyard and my father's plans for increased tourism will complement each other. Instead of appealing only to wine connoisseurs, a visitor centre that leads people on from my vineyard to other attractions will bring in a wider, though still discerning audience. I intend all my staff to be my ambassadors, and that means they must look the part. When I host my first banquet here as Count, the head of every one of my departments will attend. It's going to be a prestigious evening, so you will all be expected to look as good as these surroundings.' He looked around his stylish office with satisfaction. 'Particularly you, Meg, as you will be showing my guests that tropical wonderland you're developing.'

Meg began to relax. If all his staff were to be treated alike, she could accept something as simple as a dress allowance with no qualms.

'I got the idea from some background research I did, after my people handed me the file they'd opened on you,' Gianni went on. 'A hundred years ago, English aristocrats used to give their grandest guests a tour of the kitchen garden. Did you know that?'

'Yes…' Meg said uncertainly, not sure where this was leading. 'But this is modern Italy,' she added, remembering how keen Gianni was on looking forward rather than back.

'I know. I've spent my whole life trying to escape from the old-fashioned image of the Bellinis. Now I've shouldered all my ancient responsibilities, I'm looking for ways to make life here more bearable for myself. The old counts never simply sat around on the foothills of their wealth. They all scaled the heights, and I'm no exception. I've turned a few dozen hectares of run-down vineyard into the nucleus of a multimillion-pound business. I did it to make myself independent from my family's wealth. I've got nothing to prove in that direction. Now I've started looking into the idea of producing other local specialities. The Castelfino estate also produces top quality local food and olive oil. I want to make this villa into a beautiful place to do business with my friends and associates. They can all come and see how it's done, and help local trade at the same time. That's why I've started targeting my social life so ruthlessly. After my trophy head gardener has shown my guests around the grounds, they will be treated to a lavish banquet. Everything that can possibly be supplied by the Castelfino estate will be on display: food, wine, your flowers…everything I'm most proud of is going to be shown to its best advantage. So I want you to make as spectacular an impression on my guests as my house and grounds, Megan.'

CHAPTER FOUR

MEG loved his idea, in theory. In practice, she felt the sort of parties thrown by a social butterfly like Gianni would be as nerve-racking for her as a week at the Chelsea Flower Show.

'I can't argue with that,' she said tactfully.

'I'm *so* glad, Megan.' He gave her a knowing smile. 'In which case, you can take the rest of the day off to go and find something suitable to wear.'

Meg moved uneasily in her seat. She didn't have much experience of clothes-buying. Money had always been in short supply at home so she tended to buy things with an eye to durability rather than fashion.

'There's no need to waste a lovely afternoon shopping. I'll go into town on my next day off.'

Gianni looked pleasantly surprised at this, but Meg's next words definitely didn't impress him.

'Or...I can make do with the skirt and jacket I arrived in,' she said with a flash of relief at the thought she might avoid shopping altogether. 'It looks nice and official.'

Gianni gasped. 'Megan! It's *black*!' he said incredulously. 'That's fine for meetings, but I'm organising a banquet. And *nobody* on my staff "makes do". You'll need something new and spectacular…hmm, in the same shade of blue as your eyes, I think. Yes—that would set off the rest of your colouring perfectly. As for the style—the skirt you wore the day you arrived was good. *Very* good,' he repeated with relish. 'It showed off your legs to great effect.'

'Neither you, nor your visitors should be interested in my legs,' Meg said stiffly.

'I'm a man. But, then, you noticed that a long time ago, didn't you?' Gianni countered her disapproving expression with a winning smile. 'You are my only female head of department. I must have some small consolations in my life. To see you holding court dressed like a princess will make up for leaving the clubs of Florence behind me, and filling my home with overweight, boring businessmen, Megan.'

When he said that, Meg's common sense almost flew out of the window. It took every ounce of her will-power not to fall for his line. She knew he must spin similar stories to a new girl every night. But that was so hard to remember when his words, and the way he looked directly into her eyes as he spoke them, combined with those richly Mediterranean looks. She had to keep reminding herself that it was all part of a devastating plot. Gianni was putting her at her ease, softening her up before he moved in for the kill…

Meg knew she would have to try and turn his interest to her advantage. With a supreme effort, she forced out a few coherent words.

'Acting as an ambassador for you will be a great opportunity to show my skills to a wider audience. I'll be able to network with people who can be useful to us both. I think it's a great idea, Gianni. Do you have any other suggestions about what I should wear?'

For the second time in as many minutes he was visibly

surprised by her words. His scrutiny became slightly less seductive, but much more wary.

'Hmm…I'm beginning to think I may have misjudged you, Megan. If you're so uncertain about clothes, you need specialist advice. I'm not running the risk of you turning up in chain-store chic, no matter how *chic* that can be. A girl like you may be able to make a potato sack look sexy, but that's not the point. When I hold a party, the Villa Castelfino is out to impress. The extra sheen designer labels can give you will be well worth seeing.'

He stood up and went around to sit behind his desk again. After making a quick request through his intercom, he folded his hands on his desk. In that position he looked every inch the successful businessman. Meg could only marvel at the transformation from seducer to tycoon, but nothing could stop his true spirit gleaming through his patina of ruthless efficiency for long.

'There—I've had the best shops in Florence put on standby. I've got accounts with all these…' opening a drawer in his desk, he pulled out an indexed folder and dropped it onto his blotter '…and I send women in there all the time to treat themselves to pretty things,' he said airily.

Meg hoped he meant business-wear for the girls from his outer office. The secret smile playing around his lips as he peeled the top copy from a pile of papers made her doubt that very much.

'Any one of these places will soon fix you up with something sexy but suitable.'

He slid a single sheet of paper across the desk towards her. Meg picked it up and looked at the neatly printed list of designer names. The only place she had seen them before was in glossy magazines in the dentist's waiting room back in England. She stared at it, wondering how she would have the nerve to cross the threshold of any of the shops on his list.

'Any thoughts?' he said nonchalantly.

Meg didn't know how to put them into words. Her parents' debts had indirectly cost her the job of her dreams. Now she had worked her way up to an even better career, was it going to bankrupt her?

'All these places sound pretty…exclusive,' she said carefully.

'You don't think I'd bother opening accounts with anywhere less than perfect?'

Meg pursed her lips. She had managed to persuade Gianni not to sack her once. If she disagreed with him over this, he might change his mind. Her fear of snooty shop assistants looking down on her fought with her terror of poverty. She had seen how that could wreck lives. It wasn't something she could face a second time. Her wages for working on the Castelfino estate meant she would be able to send impressive amounts of money home each month. Although the Imsey family's plant centre was thriving now, Meg knew how narrow the line was between comfort and disaster. Her mother and father had teetered along that tightrope for too long in the past. She wanted to make sure they had plenty of funds to withstand whatever life might throw at them in the future. This job was a magnificent opportunity to build up a nest egg for them. That way, she could be sure bankruptcy wasn't lurking around every corner.

'Of course not—and that's what worries me,' she confessed. 'I need every penny of my wages. Shops like the ones on this list probably charge a fee for looking in their windows!'

Gianni leaned across his desk toward her, wrinkling his brow. 'That's what accounts are for, Megan. Everything will be charged to me. You won't pay a cent.' He used the slow, carefully enunciated speech usually reserved for speaking to small children.

She almost collapsed with relief. Then she realised she might be walking straight into a trap. The bait was sweet as honey, but she had one exceptionally good reason not to take it. Exactly how thankful would Gianni expect her to be? Her body wanted to get closer to him, there was no denying that. This would give him the ideal opportunity to tempt her further. That was why her mind was determined to hold her back. Her experiences with ex-boyfriend Gavin had given her a taste of what some men were like. She knew from experience that a man who spent money on a woman thought he had a say in her life. Accepting Gianni's generosity might lead to all sorts of things...

She looked once again into the deep, dark pools of sensuality that were his eyes. There wouldn't be any harm in accepting his generosity, her body cooed. A smile was already warming her face as she raised her eyes from the list in her hand.

'That's more than I ever expected, and very kind of you, Gianni,' she said, and was rewarded with a laugh that enclosed her in a warm, protective force field. It gave her enough courage to face the curiosity of his fearsomely glamorous assistants in the outer office again. Assuming her audience with him was finished, she stood up. As she turned to go he checked his watch.

'Wait—I'm about to leave for the Florence office. I can

give you a lift. While I'm busy, you can shop. We'll meet up again afterwards, and I'll bring you home.'

Meg stopped. Those few words sent her into total meltdown. Time alone with Gianni in his office was one thing. Travelling with him was something else.

'Fine, b-but I'll need to change first!' she stammered, already halfway to the door.

'There's no time. You look great as you are,' he announced, although Meg noticed he didn't actually look at her as he said it.

'And then there's my work—I can't just disappear without telling my staff what's happening, Gianni! Why don't you arrange a car, while I go back and leave some instructions for the men?'

He grinned and pulled a jangling collection of keys from his pocket. 'Oh, no, you don't! I know all there is to know about women. If I don't keep my eyes on you, you'll head straight for Garden Cottage and spend the next two hours delaying me while you get ready. I'll come with you, every step of the way.'

Meg wasn't about to stop him. His presence at her shoulder kept her nerves singing with anticipation. He shadowed her as she went back to the kitchen garden and completed all her meticulous checks. All the time, Meg knew he was watching. She felt his gaze running over her like quicksilver. It only slid away whenever she tried to catch his eye.

'What is happening to Imsey's Plant Centre while you are enjoying yourself here in Italy?' he said as they walked out through the garden gates and went to find his car.

'I ring home every day to find out. On my mobile, of course,' Meg added hurriedly so he wouldn't think she was running up a bill on the estate account. 'Mum and Dad say they are coping, but I'm still worried. I'm afraid they don't tell me everything. That's what happened last time.' She bit her lip.

'It seems strange to take a job far away from home when you're so devoted to them.' Gianni snapped off a tall stem of ornamental grass in passing and rubbed the embryo grains between his fingers.

'I had to.' Meg stared at the seed head in his hands, remembering. 'When your father offered me this job, it was the perfect opportunity. Helping them so successfully gave me the confidence to look for another challenge. I could strike out on my own, and begin building my career afresh.'

Her words slowed as she thought back to the one thing that had really kick started her new life. It was the night at Chelsea, when she had first met Gianni. For weeks afterwards she had fantasised about him. Then her life had turned upside down with the offer of this job, and now she was walking through a Tuscan estate beside him. It was a dream come true…almost. She tried not to notice the sunshine glittering over his raven-dark hair, or the beautiful cast of his features. It was becoming really difficult to keep work at the forefront of her mind.

'I'd secured Mum and Dad's business, and it was my time to shine again,' she added, dragging herself back to reality.

'And then out of the blue I received your father's letter, giving me the chance to pitch for the position of his Curator of Exotic Plants. He'd been impressed with me. We spent a very long time talking together at the flower show. I never dreamed you were related, but, thinking about it, that must have been his handwriting in your notebook.'

'That's right. He sent me to seek you out, so he must have been impressed.' Gianni nodded.

'Mum and Dad said they didn't need my help any more at the nursery, so here I am.'

They reached his car. The sleek black Ferrari crouched on the gravel like a wild cat. It was a great distraction from her problems, and she couldn't resist smiling.

'I'd never been close to anything like this until I came to Italy,' she breathed.

'Why? What do you drive?'

'I don't—not in this country. I'd be petrified of driving on the wrong side—I mean on the *opposite* side of the road.' She corrected herself quickly in response to the scornful look Gianni shot at her.

'Then it's time you got some practice.'

Without another word he tossed his jangling set of keys and passes at her. Meg bent to pick them up. He leaned against the passenger door with a knowing look on his face.

'You want me to drive your car?' She gasped.

'Everyone who lives in the country must drive. It's best if you start right now. And I'm only going to let you pilot her the few kilometres across my estate to the public road. I'm not completely insane.'

'But what happens if I crash it?'

He looked at her as though she were the mad one. 'I'll get the factory to send me another, of course. There's an inexhaustible supply, or so they told me the last time. And don't change the subject. We were talking about you. I thought you said you were happy at home?' he mocked, as though exposing some hypocrisy in the way she had left England. 'It didn't take much to set you on the path to fame and fortune again, did it?'

'If you had been listening carefully, you would have understood what I meant.' Meg's cheeks flared as she got into his car and tried to find a comfortable driving position. He looked puzzled. Then understanding brought his smile out of the shadows.

'You were *quite* happy, but not *completely*.' He nodded. 'Something was missing from your life.'

Someone…Meg thought. There was a pain beneath her ribs, interfering with her breathing. It was the same feeling she had endured back in England, every time she spotted someone in the distance who might have been Gianni, or thought she heard his laughter. Her heart rode a roller coaster each time it happened. She had thought no disappointment could have been greater than never seeing him a second time. But meeting him again had been more agonising than any mistake made in a shopping mall. She sensed that deep down he was suspicious of her motives.

'I wanted to make a success of my life on my own terms…' she said with difficulty.

'I can relate to that.'

His reply held such feeling Meg instantly needed to know more. Before she could ask, Gianni launched a list of instructions at her for starting his car and coaxing it toward the road.

She didn't have a hope. It was her very first driving lesson all over again, scary and embarrassing all at once. She clung onto the leather bound steering wheel in grim determination as they kangaroo-hopped down the drive. That was more than Gianni could bear. After thirty seconds he slapped both hands down on the dashboard.

'No, no—stop!'

Meg was so relieved, her emergency stop would have

passed any driving test with distinction. Gianni jumped out the second she braked. Rounding the bonnet at high speed, he opened the driver's door for her to get out.

'I'll get my office to arrange a few driving lessons to get you used to the local conditions, and then organize a car for you.' He said succinctly as he slipped into the driving seat.

Meg walked around and got in beside him. He was already caressing the steering wheel with both hands. Meg thought nothing of it, imagining he was waiting for her to fasten her seat belt, but he continued for some seconds after she was settled. Then he did all the things he had told her to do, faultlessly and in exactly the right order.

'Have I done any damage?' she risked as the upholstery surged forward against the small of her back.

'Only to my nerves.' Gianni glanced at her before checking his rear-view mirror. 'Cars are like women. They must be treated with care and respect.'

'I'm sorry,' she said in a small voice. 'I'll pay for anything that needs to be fixed.'

He laughed, loosening up as his Ferrari hit the *autostrada*. 'I think working for the Bellini family will extract a high enough price!'

'I liked your father. He was a good employer,' Meg said, filling every word with meaning.

'And you're hoping I'll carry on the family tradition, *bambola*?' Gianni slipped the words slyly across at her. 'I doubt that. I'm entirely different from my father. For one thing, he had been desperate to marry. It turned out to be the worst mistake he ever made, and I've learned from it. When my mother died in childbirth it was the ultimate irony. The whole experience damaged him so badly he spent thirty years licking his wounds. I intend to take my time choosing a bride. Not for me the flighty socialite, ready to bleed me dry in the name of marriage,' he finished darkly.

'I think you're very wise.'

'Really?' he drawled, grinning across the car's interior at her. 'And is that the only reason you accepted this lift? It wouldn't be because you were thinking of renegotiating your terms of employment, would it?'

The look he gave Meg then told her exactly what he meant by that. His mind, like hers, was savouring their kiss all over again. The warmth of his expression spoke to the deepest, darkest parts of her. She reacted with a furious blush, and the knowledge that she would never be free from the temptation of Gianni for as long as she lived.

'While I'm living at the Villa Castelfino, I'm not remotely interested in anything other than work,' she announced, being careful to stare at the countryside rather than look at him. 'When I mentioned about getting paid for turning up ready for work you looked at me as though I was a gold digger. What illusions could I possibly have about a man who treats an employee like that on her first day?'

The taboo subject of money had been mentioned again. Every muscle in Meg's body tensed. For an awful minute she thought Gianni might throw her out of the car for being hard-hearted and interested only in her bank balance. When he didn't, she began pulling her fingers through the wind-whipped tangle of her hair. It was easier to worry about her appearance than to apologise.

Out of the corner of her eye she saw Gianni shrug. 'It's a shame more women don't think like you do. All the girls

I meet are out for everything they can get. I'm definitely *not* looking for the same kind of woman who ruined my father's life, and mine. So far, I've been proud to say I'm not the marrying kind.'

'I hope you never used that phrase on any woman when you lived in England. It has a meaning there you wouldn't like,' Meg warned.

He winced. 'Of course I didn't. In any case, once a woman is with me, she knows I'm one hundred per cent male.'

At that moment he turned another unmistakeable look on her. It was rich with lingering meaning. Meg had to fight the urge to reach right out and touch him. Then she saw the juggernaut thundering towards them and snatched at her seat instead.

'Gianni! Look out!'

'*Inferno*, woman! Do you think I would risk an accident now? In my new car, I mean?' he added quickly, before she could read any more temptation in his words.

Gianni was careful to drop her off at the nearest possible point to the first shop on her list. Ignoring all the blaring horns around them, he parked his car, got out and opened the passenger door for her.

'How much would you like for a tip?' she asked mischievously as she unfolded herself from the front seat.

'I'll let you have it on account.'

Meg's heart almost stopped as she saw his watchful expression. When he caught up her hand and kissed it, she was speechless. If he hadn't leapt straight back into his car and roared away, she would have thrown herself into his arms then and there. Breathless with amazement, she stood on the pavement and stared, long after his car had turned a corner and disappeared from view. An afternoon off to take her pick of clothes from some of the world's most decadent shops was one thing. For Gianni to kiss her hand the same way he had done at Chelsea was a dream beyond anything Meg had ever imagined. She felt inches taller, and even began to look forward to her shopping expedition. The man was a miracle worker.

Meg usually looked on shopping as a torture. This was a different outing altogether. Today she was under Gianni's instructions to buy something she really liked, while he picked up the bill. She usually bustled through crowds, head down and hurrying. Today she strolled, taking time to enjoy her afternoon off in the sun. The touch of his lips still tingled on her fingers. Only one tiny cloud lingered on her horizon. It was the thought of what embarrassments might lay in wait for her inside the beautiful shops she would be visiting.

It took her quite some time to pluck up the courage to put her hand to the door of the first boutique on her list. After that, things happened in such a blur she didn't have time to lose her nerve. The door flew open as a tall, stick-thin woman decorated with twenty-four carat jewellery strode out. Meg was bundled aside in the rush but a voice from inside the shop was quick to apologise.

'Miss Imsey?'

She looked up in amazement to see an exquisitely turned out Florentine matron holding the door open for her.

'H-how did you know it was me?' Meg stammered.

'The Count di Castelfino himself rang to tell us to expect you. Now come inside out of this heat!'

Meg was made to feel at home instantly, despite all the designer labels. She was almost disappointed to find the perfect dress within minutes. It was a close fitting sheath of sky-blue moiré. Sleeveless and low cut with a matching jacket, it would make the most of her newly acquired tan. The assistant helped her choose an outrageously high pair of silk slingbacks to complement the outfit, and promised they would be dyed to match in time for Gianni's party. Strutting through a gallery of full-length mirrors, Meg marvelled at her transformation. She felt like a million dollars, and the effect on her was obvious. She glowed. It was amazing—this outfit took pounds off her, and gave her so much confidence! She had never dreamed she could look so good. For the first time she revelled in her own reflection. Instead of seeing Gianni's coming banquet as a terrifying ordeal, she actually began to look forward to the experience. Expansive with self-confidence, she cheerfully announced that she would take the dress and the shoes, which should all be charged to the Count di Castelfino's account.

The manageress shook her head gravely.

'Not yet, madam. I was instructed to ask how many shops you have visited so far before agreeing to sell you anything.'

'This is the first,' Meg answered honestly, but soon wished she hadn't. A second assistant gently lifted the beautiful blue outfit from her hands and whisked it away to a back room.

'Don't worry. We'll keep it safe for you. But knowing the new count, it is as well to follow his instructions to the letter.'

Meg could believe it. Her heart sank. All she wanted to do was get back to her little house on the Villa Castelfino estate. It was the only place in this foreign land she felt truly comfortable. She understood all there was to know about plants, but shopping was a mystery she'd never had enough money to investigate before. It was made only slightly less nerve-racking by the fact that Gianni would be paying.

'Oh, no…does that mean I have to do this all over again, from top to bottom of the city?' She stared at the sheet of paper Gianni had given her. Her face was as long as his list.

'It may not be so bad, madam. Try to put a brave face on it,' the assistant sympathised. Her words brought Meg straight back to her senses.

'Good grief, to hear me talk anyone would think this was hard work! If all I've got to do to please him is to rifle through a few clothes racks, I'll be finished in no time!' she announced.

Things didn't go quite according to Meg's master plan. She swept in and out of the next shop at high speed, but as she progressed down the list each visit became longer, and more leisurely. Although she never found anything that suited her taste and Gianni's instructions as perfectly as the blue sheath and jacket, she actually began to enjoy herself. All the shop assistants fawned around her as though she were royalty. She was offered drinks, sweets and snacks everywhere she went. Trying on clothes became a delight rather than a chore. She learned that rich fabrics needed to be enjoyed and lingered over, not pulled on and off at speed. When she got to the final establishment on her list, she was amazed to find it was a real wrench to leave. But at last, awash with coffee and stuffed with cantuccini, she returned to seal the deal on her ideal outfit.

* * *

She had arranged to meet Gianni near the Ponte Vecchio. He was already there, laughing into his mobile. The moment the weight of his gaze fell on her, he ended the call. Walking towards her with a smile, he pulled out his car keys.

'You haven't taken as long as I thought you would!' His gaze ran over her, and Meg's mouth went dry. The afternoon was so hot she'd been convinced her temperature couldn't possibly climb any higher. She was wrong. He looked magnificent. The contrast between his olive colouring and the brilliant white shirts he favoured was one she always admired. Today she was in for an extra treat. Gianni had not only turned back his cuffs so they exposed his smooth tanned forearms, he had also taken off his tie, and there were enough buttons open at his neck to expose a dark shadow of hair. Meg's pulse began to race away with her manners. It was all she could do to keep either under control.

'Don't worry, Gianni. I've got everything for the business banquet, exactly as you instructed. Thank you so much. And would you believe it—I got most of it only after I ended up back at the *very first shop* I visited! They're going to deliver it as soon as all the alterations have been made. Now—let's get back to the villa. I can't wait to get home, kick off my shoes and—'

She stopped, painfully aware she was gabbling. Gianni raised his eyes to heaven and clicked his tongue.

'Women! If they're at home they want to be out shopping. If they're out and about, they want to get back home! They're all the same!' he said in a voice full of Italian indulgence.

I'm not. How I'd love to linger here with you. Oh, if only you knew… Meg thought, but bit her tongue. It wasn't the first time, and it wouldn't be the last.

The days before Gianni's first formal banquet passed in a whirl of preparations.

'I knew I made the right decision in employing a female head gardener,' he announced innocently as Meg knelt on a hearth, working at a flower arrangement. When he said that she sat back on her heels.

'So you weren't the man who threatened me with redundancy the moment I arrived?' she mocked, without looking at him.

Gianni ignored her comment. He was too busy surveying the floral decorations draped around the summer dining hall. 'I ask you—what man could have done this so beautifully?'

'My great-great-grandfather and his contemporaries, for a start,' Meg said, adding an extra spray of tiny orchid flowers to the display of lichen- and moss-encrusted logs set in the fireplace. She had designed everything, from the colour schemes to the hand-tied bouquets. It had given her so much pleasure. Gianni's praise more than doubled her satisfaction, and she smiled as she put the finishing touches to the floral fire in the empty hearth. It was a sparkling mass of red and gold flowers, all cosseted in the perfect environment of the estate's brand-new greenhouses. That was an extra source of pride for Meg. She had done it all herself.

'Years ago floral art was part of every head gardener's job description, no matter how tough and manly he was,' she continued. 'Going even further back, it was a prized skill among samurai swordsmen in Japan.'

'I'd prefer geishas myself.'

'I'm sure you would.' Meg half turned to shoot the remark over her shoulder. The sight that met her eyes brought her up short. Although there was still some time to go before his guests were due to arrive, Gianni was already in full evening dress. He looked magnificent. Every inch the tenth generation aristocrat, he surveyed her work with pride. Meg couldn't help staring up at him in barely concealed wonder. He grinned.

'Flattering though your expression is, you don't have time to crouch in the hearth, Cinderella! Your big moment starts in under an hour, and I want all my staff ready on time.'

Meg got to her feet slowly. It wasn't often she had the chance to get so close to Gianni. She relished this rare excuse. Brushing the creases from her clothes added a few moments to her time in his presence. She was in no hurry to leave. He soon noticed.

'I get the impression you aren't looking forward to this.'

Meg made a face. Her mind had been full of all sorts of things but he had picked up on a particular worry. She decided there was nothing to lose by being frank.

'I'm dreading it, to be perfectly honest.'

'So am I.'

She stopped dead and stared at him, incredulous. There were only three other words this man was less likely to say, and they were *I love you*. His response had been so unexpected, she almost laughed.

'But you're the original socialite! How can you be dreading a party?' she mocked. 'I don't believe it!'

Gianni was engrossed in removing a stray thread from his sleeve. When he heard the amusement in her voice he looked up.

'This isn't a party. This is work, Megan. To my mind

the two things don't go together at all. Once upon a time I could afford to relax. Now I'm responsible for the whole of the Castelfino estate and its employees, I can't miss any opportunity to push the brand forward.'

He sounded so grim, Meg shivered.

'Then thank goodness I have a job I love!' she said with such feeling he laughed. The next moment he had closed the gap between them. Patting her shoulder, he gave a reassuring smile especially for her.

'Don't worry, Megan. It'll be fine. You'll see.'

Meg couldn't share Gianni's confidence. It took her no time at all to shower and change into her party clothes, but then her worries began in earnest. She dithered over which perfume to choose, and whether or not to wear lipstick. It was a classic case of putting off the moment when she would have to leave home. Only the memory of Gianni's smile and his comforting words drew her out of her sanctuary. By the time she left her cottage the first vehicle was already visible in the distance, coming through the estate's main gates.

'*Bravissimo*—you look stunning.'

A warmly welcome voice descended on Meg from above, making her jump.

'Gianni!'

Looking up, she saw him leaning over the wrought-iron balustrade of an upstairs balcony. Her stomach leapt as she remembered what he had said about watching her from his window. The darkness behind him must be his bedroom. Still warm and fragrant from her shower, Meg's body began fizzing with unusual excitement.

'W-what are you doing up there?' she said, trying to disguise the depth of her need to know.

'Waiting for you to appear, of course. Another ten seconds, and I would have sent out a search party.'

His admiring look made her bold.

'You're such a devoted employer, Gianni, I thought you'd be only too keen to take on the job yourself.'

He wrinkled his nose in disdain at the idea. 'No, certainly not. Any visit to Garden Cottage would deserve time I don't have at the moment. If I undertake a task, I follow it right through to the end.'

His voice was slow and deep with meaning. Until that moment Meg had been convinced her desire for him would never be allowed to come to anything. Now she saw her destiny. It was written in his eyes, and her temperature went off the scale. Only one thing would satisfy her now, and he knew. She saw it in his stance and his confident attitude. He was totally at home, and at ease with himself. It was the best aphrodisiac Meg could wish for.

A hot breeze rustled among the ornamental bamboos. It carried the sound of expensive engines prowling closer by the second.

'I—I must get to my place in the greenhouse.' She backed away towards the kitchen garden, wanting to keep eye contact with him until the last possible moment. His lips parted in the famous Bellini smile, an inheritance that surely must have spelled disaster for dozens of girls.

'Don't worry, *mio dolce*,' he said with leisurely confidence. 'I won't be starting without you.'

CHAPTER FIVE

MEG had been on pins all day. It was her job to show Gianni's guests around the restored kitchen garden and the new greenhouses, before the banquet. How to keep calm among dozens of wealthy and glamorous guests was the last thing on her mind now. As she waited to welcome the first visitors into her workplace, her mind was feverish with possibilities. Other aristocrats and billionaires meant nothing to her. All she could think about was their host.

While she was stuck out here in the grounds, Gianni was inside greeting his guests. He was within forty metres of her, but she wouldn't be able to catch so much as a glimpse of him yet. She shut her eyes and imagined what was going on inside the house. Every inch the rich, pampered play-boy, Gianni would be charming everyone. She knew exactly how he would look, the warmth of those fathomless dark eyes, the perfection of his skin, and the contrast with his even white teeth. Her body lurched with desire for him, and her eyes flew open with the sensation.

In desperation she tried to focus on the ordeal ahead. All the time she was counting down the seconds until she could see Gianni again. She already knew the dining hall's seating plan off by heart. She had been placed opposite him, and between two of the most important local business-men. It was her job, along with all the other heads of department employed by the Castelfino estate, to persuade them to join Gianni's local suppliers' scheme. He would be working his own particular brand of magic on two other dignitaries on the other side of the table. One of them was a Signora Ricci. Without knowing a thing about the woman, Meg's instinct was to hate her. To deserve an invitation to Gianni's stellar event the woman had to be rich and well connected. What if she was beautiful and charming as well? Already green with jealousy, Meg retreated to the place where she felt safest. Roaming restlessly through the glasshouses, she checked her watch. There was an hour to wait until they were summoned in to dinner. Meg didn't know how she was going to stand the suspense.

She need not have worried. When the first visitors straggled in through the gate to her kitchen garden, pride overwhelmed her. She was so busy trying to give everyone a glowing account of the work in progress the time flew past. It was in everyone's interests that the evening went well. Gianni had a lot of money riding on the result. Meg's job might well be at stake too, and she was determined to make a success of her life. She didn't intend disappointing herself, or anyone else.

To her relief, no one shared Gianni's opinion of greenhouses as an expensive, outdated luxury. Not one of them mentioned the words 'carbon footprint'. They all loved the exotic displays she had built and the luxurious feeling of walking through a rainforest. Meg felt vindicated, and relieved. When the time came to shepherd the last few guests in towards dinner, she had an extra reason for needing to see Gianni. She couldn't wait to tell him how well everything had gone. The hot summer evening and that vision of him on his balcony had sent all her fears of making another mistake into a black hole of desire. Her body now hungered for him more than any food. She was glowing with arousal as well as success.

The ground floor of the villa teemed with hundreds of people. Meg scanned the crowds, searching for that one unmistakeable figure. When she saw him, she smiled with recognition at the image. He was working the room, and looked effortlessly impressive. Uniformed waiters moved smoothly through the crowds, ensuring the champagne flowed like water. Huge silver salvers of canapés were circulating, and no one was allowed to stand around empty-handed. Gianni was the most generous host, and his famous charm kept the party mood buoyant. Meg had all of five seconds to watch him doing what he did best before her ordeal began. The dinner gong sounded, and the waiters began showing everyone towards the lofty splendour of the summer dining room. Although everyone smiled at her and many men gestured for her to go ahead of them, Meg shook her head. She hung back, careful to let all the grand guests go in to dinner before her.

Suddenly Gianni was at her side. 'What's the matter?'

It was such a relief to stop smiling for the guests, Meg couldn't help letting her true feelings show.

'I feel so awkward! I don't know anyone!' she muttered. He dismissed her attitude with a wave of his hand.

'You know *me*, and that's all that matters.'

He flipped the edges of his jacket, momentarily showing off his expertly fitted waistcoat and snowy white shirt beneath. Meg's heart jumped. All the polite, charming and witty things she had been planning to say to him fled from her mind. She was left gazing at him in wonder. His crisp shirt accentuated the fine colour of his skin and the darkness of his eyes. He smiled at her, showing his beautifully white, even teeth. Meg felt a tingle of anticipation. Then with a jolt she saw she wasn't the only one. Behind Gianni's politely formal expression she sensed something very different. It was raw, naked desire. Her senses spun out of control. Suddenly she wanted to stride forward, push her fingers through his unruly tousle of curls and experience his kisses again, no questions asked.

Instead she blushed, dropped her gaze, and shuffled uncertainly on the spot. Gianni knew exactly how to reward such touching allure. He took a few lazy steps forward and cupped her chin with his hand.

Meg raised her head. Their eyes connected in a look that was totally out of place in such a high-class setting. But Gianni Bellini thought nothing of convention. He levelled a look at Meg that dared her to move. She could not. Instead she relished the touch of his fingers as they slid along the line of her jaw. His touch was strong, yet cool. If it had been any other man she would have pulled away. This was different. She smiled, and so did he.

'I've never seen a lovelier woman,' he purred. 'Or one so beautifully dressed.'

Meg opened her mouth to say something, but those words turned her mind to jelly. Brushing her free hand over the silken folds of her new clothes, she tried another smile. Luckily, those muscles were still working despite the effect Gianni was having on the rest of her body. She could only hope her expression spoke for her.

She smiled at the idea.

'That's better! You don't need anything more than a

smile to make you the loveliest woman in the universe, Megan.'

Her heart sank as his touch left her, but he could not keep his hands off her for long. He took her arm, his fingers running slowly over her sleeve until they reached her hand. Then he inclined his head towards the summer dining room. 'And now, Miss Imsey, shall we…?'

'I'd be delighted, Signor Bellini.' Meg smiled, and meant it.

Her mind was in a whirl as Gianni led her towards the banquet. The nearness of him acted on her like a drug. How was she supposed to make polite conversation over dinner when she felt like this? She was so nervous she could barely glance at him, but tried to look on the bright side. Her shyness was because he was so gorgeous. He was the most handsome man she had ever seen. *And it feels as though he's pretty impressed with me tonight, too,* she thought, and blushed. What would he think if he knew that, despite her determined stand against his liquid eyes and irresistible hands, his gaze and touch still filled her mind? She was already fantasising about kissing him again. As she did so she coloured guiltily, and he noticed.

'Don't hang back! What's the matter? I hope none of my male guests tried to distract you while you were showing them around your tropical empire?'

Her heartbeat increased. There was only one person in the world who could distract her, and that was him.

'Don't tell me that old dog Alterra has been up to his tricks again?' Gianni said with sudden vigour.

'No! Everyone has treated me very well. I was a bit

worried that Italy would be full of bottom-pinching Don Giovannis, but luckily that turned out to be nothing but a—'

She stopped with a squeal, her eyes wide with surprise. Gianni's hand had slithered over her rump and delivered an intimate squeeze. In between smiling and nodding at his guests as they passed on their way in to dinner, he leaned in close and whispered in Meg's ear.

'It would be *such* a shame if every single man here tonight let the side down, *mio dolce*!' he murmured. With a mischievous wink he detached himself from her, ready to take his place at the main table.

Meg couldn't help herself.

'Don't leave me, Gianni!' The cry escaped before she could stifle it. 'I'm not cut out for this!'

'Of course you are!' His hand darted out to her again, but this time he gave her nothing more than a friendly pat of reassurance. 'Come and sit down. Remember how impressed I was by you at the Chelsea Flower Show? Think about your spectacular triumph there. Concentrate on your achievements, not your doubts. If all else fails, count your qualifications,' he finished with dry humour. Suddenly he leaned forward until his breath was whispering right into her ear. 'You've got more to be proud of than all these *celebrità* put together!' he murmured. Then he squeezed her elbow, and was gone.

Meg's mouth fell open. Could that possibly be true? Her mind reeled through everything Gianni had ever said to her. Her body had burned for him from that first meeting at Chelsea. Now she was fired up for quite another reason. She had a job to do, and it was one full of purpose. By helping Gianni push forward with his plans for the

Castelfino Estate, she would be securing her own future here at the villa. She might even earn some special thanks from him...

His flattery worked. Meg walked through the banqueting hall with her head held high, full of his encouragement. As she scanned the crowds of Europe's most influential people only one man could hold her gaze. Gianni was in his element. Tall and suave, he stood behind his chair at the centre of the fifteen-metre long dining table, chatting with everyone. Meg hungered for another taste of his skill at putting people at their ease. She could not wait to take the empty place opposite him, but the crowd in front of her moved with agonising slowness. They were more interested in the life-sized Bellini family portraits ranged around the walls. Meg had to content herself with watching Gianni from a distance as he entertained his audience like the professional he was. She didn't have long to savour his skill. He must have felt her watching him because suddenly he stopped, and shot a smile straight at her.

'Ladies and Gentlemen—please give a special vote of thanks to the Villa Castelfino's head gardener—Miss Megan Imsey. On top of her usual duties, she is responsible for all the wonderful floral art you see around you tonight!' With that, he began to clap. His audience joined in. They all turned patronising smiles on Meg as she stood in the spotlight, shimmering with nerves.

She could have died from embarrassment, but cringing wasn't an option tonight. *Gianni likes my work so much he's telling everyone. Perhaps I'm as good as he says I am, after all!* She told herself. Nailing on a broad smile, she stood up as tall as she could and flung back her shoulders.

The gaggle of guests blocking her way parted like magic. That gave her the confidence to stride straight towards the table. A footman pulled out her chair as she arrived. As she sat down he took the starched napkin from her side plate. Shaking out its folds, he settled it on her lap. Gianni watched the whole performance with undisguised pleasure.

'I said you would be the star of my show, Megan,' he murmured.

A portly, florid-faced couple waddled up to take their seats at the table, interrupting before Meg could respond with anything more than a nervous laugh.

'Can't you leave the girls alone for a single minute, Gianni?' the man wheezed cheerfully.

'When are you going to settle down under a mountain of debt and responsibility, like us?' the woman added as she took the seat next to Gianni. This must be the Signora Ricci whom Meg had imagined to be a teenaged supermodel. Instead, she was an elderly woman wearing inches of make-up and weighing close to twenty stone. Meg heaved a huge sigh of relief. Despite Signora Ricci's supercilious expression, Meg gave her a particularly warm smile. Gianni cleared his throat. Always glad of an excuse to look at him, Meg glanced across the table. He fixed her with an amused smile, but the look in his eyes was penetrating. 'Never, if I have any say in the matter!'

His expression almost took Meg's breath away. There could be no doubt about it—he meant what he said. This was a stark reminder. Giving her a conspiratorial wink, he greeted the newcomers with his special brand of charm. Meg tried not to look. But she couldn't help listening in to the conversation, and was soon overwhelmed with a mixture of shock and admiration. Gianni could make all his words sound as convincing as his flirtation. She had to admire him for it. If only she could charm people so easily! She might have bounced Imsey's Plant Centre out of trouble in minutes, rather than months. That would have left her free to concentrate on her own career. She could have taken that job with the royal family…but then, if she had done that, maybe she would never have met Gianni…

'Aren't you going to introduce your latest "friend" to us properly, Gianni?' Signora Ricci boomed suddenly. She refused to be deflected from inspecting Meg, and looked at her as though she were something usually found in a spa drain. 'Though how we're expected to remember the names of all your women I really don't know. You'll have found yourself another before the evening's over, I'll bet!'

Meg didn't know what to do. She wished she could think of a stinging reply, but this company was far too important to upset. She blushed and shrank in her seat, but Gianni came straight to her rescue. He drew himself up to his full impressive height. Everyone around them gasped. At well over six feet tall, he towered over his audience. Right now he was using every inch of his powerful build to drive his message home.

'That's what you think, Signora Ricci,' he murmured, his seductive dark eyes hard as jet. 'Now I am in charge here, the Castelfino estate is my priority. Everything else takes second place. And I mean everything. When I misbehave these days, I do it in private.'

This didn't satisfy his tormentors. They guffawed loudly. 'No, you'll never change, Gianni! It's a pity your father never saw through you, and recognised the truth. Someone should have told him. All your fast living will wreck this beautiful land, and you couldn't even be bothered to give him a grandson to carry on the family name while he was alive!' Signora Ricci cackled.

Until this point Gianni had merely looked annoyed. Now Meg saw a change come over him. At the mention of his father he drew in a long, exasperated breath and raised his granite chin in defiance. A nerve pulsed in his neck. Danger flashed in the glitter of his eyes. This guest had definitely found a chink in his armour of suave sophistication. He looked down his aristocratic nose at her as he delivered a damning retort.

'That's all in hand,' He said coldly. 'As soon as my plans for the Castelfino Estate are up and running, I shall marry. And I would be grateful if you would show my head gardener a little more respect, *signora*.'

His manners were perfect, and his smile as polite as ever. Despite that, Meg saw that his body was rigid, and his knuckles were white as he gripped the back of his chair. A cocktail of alarm and dread rushed through her veins. Signora Ricci had no such fears. She laughed out loud.

'You're going to get *married*, Gianni? *You*?'

'*Naturalmente*. Tradition means everything to my family. I must have a child, whatever the cost.'

In a flash Meg saw that the price to him would be astronomical. His words were darts of barely concealed anger, puncturing Signora Ricci like a balloon. Meg wilted at his tone, even though his rage was not directed at her. The moment he noticed her reaction, he took his seat and called for wine to be poured. It was enough of a distraction to allow him to shoot a few words across the table to her without anyone else noticing.

'It's OK, Megan. Cheer up—this evening is supposed to be a chance for people to enjoy themselves, don't forget!'

When Gianni saw her smile, his temper improved in a flash. This might not be the nightclubs of Rome or New York, but it was a party, for all that. He was in his element. There was gourmet food, vintage wine and he had the most intriguing girl in the world seated opposite him. And every time he spoke to her, Meg's lovely face lit up with a promise that was reflected all through her body. Candlelight rippled over the caramel waves of her hair, making it glitter with gold. She moved like a gentle breeze, tempting him with thoughts of possible pleasures to come. His eyes were drawn back to her time and again.

She's some girl, he thought appreciatively, *and tonight she's acting the part of gracious lady to perfection*. He smiled again as she was thrown into a momentary panic. Her napkin had slithered over the slippery surface of her dress, and fallen to the floor. Lifting the damask square from his own lap, he flourished it across the table towards her in a crackle of starched linen.

'Don't worry, Megan. You can take mine.' He glittered at her. She responded with a flurry of blushes and thanks. He liked that. He never had to try when it came to impressing women, but his mind had seized on an intriguing idea. He felt the urge to turn this banquet into the equivalent of their first date. At times like this, it never hurt to go the extra mile.

That's progress! he thought, taking note of the way Meg thanked him. Dancing shadows thrown by the candlelight accentuated the tempting depths of her cleavage.

Although the room was warm, her nipples were already obvious through the silk of her dress. Gianni's temperature rose. A new idea was forming in his restless mind. She was ambitious. He wanted her body. There might be a way to satisfy them both. His polite, public smile took on considerable inner warmth. This staid business banquet had given him a very good idea. Turning from playboy to patrician was shaping up to be the best sacrifice he had made in his life.

CHAPTER SIX

MORE wine was poured. Meg looked doubtfully at the mildewed peeling label on the bottle before her. She questioned Gianni across the table with her eyes.

'It's the villa's tignanello reserve, kept for extra special occasions,' Gianni explained, skimming his spoon across the bowl of soup in front of him. 'Don't let your consommé get cold, Megan. It's too delicious to miss.' He shot a look across the table at her. His meaning was as clear as the crystal carafe of water standing between them. It said: *And so are you...*

Gianni was a dedicated playboy, and while he might not yet be interested in marriage it did seem that for now he had his sights set on an affair with her, making it clear he was hers for the taking! *He blew into my life like a tornado and wiped every other thought clean out of my mind. It's the perfect excuse. Why shouldn't I go mad, just this once? Heaven knows I deserve it. Up until now, I've sacrificed everything for the sake of my career. Surely it's time to find out exactly what I've been missing!*

She lifted her eyes and looked at Gianni across the table.

No woman can possibly be safe from him. So no one in the universe could blame me for falling under his spell…

She wavered. Then Gianni suddenly switched his attention to the pretty little waitress who had come to take his empty soup plate. The same irresistible smile was turned on her. In that instant Meg almost came to her senses. A voice in her head told her that this tiger would never settle down. She had heard it from his own lips, only a moment ago. Where did that leave her misty dreams of true love? But screams of reason, no matter how shrill, never had a chance. Meg's whole body, mind and spirit had been taken over by thoughts of Gianni. Common sense dissolved. Everything about him overwhelmed her, from the delicious fragrance of his aftershave to the lilt of his voice. She wanted him, even if he slipped away through her fingers like a sunbeam. Whatever heartbreak the future might hold, she would be sure of at least one brief moment of happiness.

In that instant, Gianni's expression changed. His eyes narrowed. A triumphant smile teased his lips. He became as watchful as a panther. Instead of being caressed by his gaze, Meg now felt invisible hands bending her to his will. The more certainty there was in Gianni's expression, the more unstable she felt. *I'm way out of my depth!* she realised desperately. *I can't allow myself to fall into the hands of a man who'll drop me in an instant! What will he think of me?*

Even as she cringed at the thought, that wicked voice of temptation called to her again. *This could be the most spectacular night of my life. If I never take a risk, I'll never know. As long as we're both discreet, where's the problem?* it said, loud and clear. The sudden rush of bravado raised her head and lowered her lashes. When she gazed across the table at Gianni now, it was with new eyes.

Delicious courses of the finest organic produce the Castelfino estate could produce came and went. Meg barely noticed. The conversation washed over her like a gentle tide. Finally, when the last pudding dish had been spirited away, more champagne arrived. Gianni pushed back his chair and stood up to give his speech. He spoke to the whole room, like the seasoned professional he was, but Meg felt every word of thanks and praise directed straight at her. He was laid-back, and delighted them all. She followed his every movement, every gesture. His gaze ranged right across the assembly but he never once made eye contact with her, however much she lusted after his attention. He announced many toasts, but barely touched his own foaming glass of Taittinger. In her nervousness, Meg emptied her glass twice. As Gianni sat down a waiter moved in to fill her glass again. The host was equally swift. Reaching across the table, he removed the crystal flute from her fingers.

'That's quite enough for tonight, don't you think? You'll need to keep your wits about you on the dance floor.'

His words wiped the smile straight from her face. 'I'd forgotten that. I was looking forward to escaping to my greenhouses,' she muttered, watching the glittering assembly with a hunted expression.

'*Whose* greenhouse?' Gianni's supercilious expression was only slightly softened when he raised his eyebrows. 'Don't worry. A couple more hours of dancing to my tune, then you'll get your reward. You promised me a deluxe tour of the new empire you've created for me out in the grounds, remember? I'm the only person who hasn't inspected Castelfino's new exotic plant ranges, ladies and gentlemen,' he explained to all the guests seated within earshot. 'This evening has been such a success I'll need some time to wind down afterwards. Would you mind if I took full advantage of your tropical paradise later on, Megan?'

His voice was as seductive as his expression. The promise in it was dark, dangerous and totally irresistible. She could only nod in reply. He smiled, his eyes flashing something that might have been triumph. Meg was on fire, but that look warned her she would have to be patient. This was Gianni's evening. His cool confidence would keep him in control—until the moment they were alone together...

Meg yearned for a touch, or a look. It was a long time in coming. She had to watch him working the room in the same way he had charmed everyone at the Chelsea Flower Show. He had a smile and a friendly word for everyone— except Meg. She developed a way of flicking glances around the ballroom while still appearing to keep her full attention on the guest who was talking to her. Meg wasn't one of life's minglers, but she could do it when necessary. Gianni was an expert, and tonight he was conducting a masterclass. By the time his circuit of the room brought him back to her, she was burning with anticipation.

'Thank goodness you're back, Gianni! I'm running out of things to say!'

'Oh, I doubt that.' He chuckled. 'You're a natural at this, Megan. I've been watching you. You've missed your vocation in life. You would have been a great addition to the English royal family.'

Blushing furiously, Meg opened her mouth to protest at his joke but Gianni waved her worries aside.

'Don't disagree with me, Meg. I don't have time for any of this "English reserve" nonsense. Diffidence never won any sales.' All the time he was speaking, Gianni was casting an eye around the ballroom. He was the perfect host to his fingertips. Although concentrating on his guests, he noticed something the moment he began guiding Meg onto the dance floor.

'It's good to know you haven't been trampling all over my clients' feet. Not many girls can dance as well as you, Meg.'

Remembering his earlier words, she accepted the compliment gracefully. 'Thank you, Gianni. It's a useful social skill.'

'And you have plenty of those. Thank you for being such a help to me this evening.' He stopped studying his guests and looked down at her. His smile was too calculating to warm his eyes, but she couldn't help reacting. Warmth flowed through her limbs like melting chocolate, slow and sweet. All the compliments she had been given about her work in the kitchen garden finally made sense. Gianni appreciated her efforts. His guests liked her work. They couldn't all be saying nice things simply to be polite. They must mean them. All the compliments on top of two glasses of champagne made it a night for bravery.

'It's all an act,' she admitted.

'*Mai!*' he laughed. 'I don't believe you. For instance, if I were to take you in my arms properly, and sweep you across the floor like this—'

With one bold movement he drew her into his body and propelled her towards the centre of the room. Other dancers melted away before them. Breathless with amazement, Meg was carried along by his expertise, held as though she were precious porcelain. Her beautiful new gown shimmered like a peacock's feathers in the glow of a thousand candles. Caught up in the moment, she looked up into his eyes and saw the chandeliers were reflected in the darkness of his eyes, too.

'Gianni…I never thought anything could feel like this…' she gasped. His smile broadened. Meg knew instinctively she had said the wrong thing. This was Gianni Bellini. His silence had led to her spilling her soul in his office. Now his firm grasp and sure footsteps were dancing her into more danger. Her mind whirled in waltz-time. Only silence could have saved her. Telling him how she felt had only confirmed his already high opinion of himself as a ladykiller. She had played right into his hands. Hating herself for melting so completely against his body, Meg still could not stop. His touch was light but so assured she was powerless to resist. While his left hand clasped hers, the fingers of his right hand spread out in a protective cage across her back. He kept up the pressure, her breasts held secure against the broad expanse of his chest as they made turn after turn around the room. Meg shone in his arms, shown to her best advantage as she followed his lead. When the final strains of Strauss died away, Meg felt her face fall with disappointment. Then the applause began. Looking around with the confusion of a sleepwalker, she realised everyone was clapping—including Gianni.

'Ladies and gentlemen: I give you the best qualified, the most nimble and the most beautiful head gardener in the history of horticulture!' he announced.

Meg threw her hands up to her face, trying to cover her embarrassment. The crowd cooed its approval, and Gianni

reached out to her. Meg looked at him with shining eyes.
All he did was pat her shoulder in a parting gesture.

'There—I said you could cope with anything!' he said
with a wink as his adoring crowd absorbed him again.

'Gianni—' Meg began, but it was hopeless. He had
moved on. Guests began reclaiming the dance floor. Soon
she was enveloped by a tide of couples. They all smiled
and nodded knowingly at her, as though she were a
marked woman from that moment on. As the band played
on Meg forced herself to walk steadily away from the
dance floor, head held high. Gianni might have taken her
to paradise, but she could not afford to have her head in
the clouds. No good ever came of mixing work with
pleasure. As a student her studies had faltered when she
had allowed Gavin to distract her. She was not going to
make the same mistake again. She couldn't afford to—in
any sense of the word. This was the best job anyone in
her position could wish for. *And it has the best employer
too,* she thought wistfully, before she could think of a
more politically correct reason. *I can't afford to mess up
this one chance of making a success in a job that really
matters to me.*

The rest of Meg's evening passed in an agony of suspense.
Simmering with the promise Gianni had shown her, she
was petrified the guests might notice something. She felt
feverish. Catching sight of a reflection in one of the huge
antique mirrors set around the summer dining hall, it was
a few seconds before she recognised herself. She was used
to seeing a dowdy little country mouse peering back at her.
Tonight she saw quite a different creature. Her new dress
and high heels made her look tall and sleek, but they were

only window dressing. Meg had blossomed to complement their designer chic. Her eyes were large and luminous, her cheeks flushed and her hair coiled around her shoulders with a life of its own.

Gianni looked as though he didn't have a care in the world. Cool and composed, he was totally absorbed by his guests. None of them was in any hurry to leave such a brilliant gathering, and he showed no signs of evicting them. Brought to fever pitch and now abandoned, Meg grew increasingly restless. Finally, she couldn't stand it any longer. If he was so busy with his guests, he obviously wasn't that bothered about her. In a flurry of indignation she set off towards the door. She had taken no more than three determined steps when Gianni appeared from nowhere and put a hand on her arm.

'And where do you think you're going, *mio tesoro*?'

His dark brows were raised. No answer was needed. The touch of his fingers on her sleeve was light, but inescapable. 'None of my staff leaves before I dismiss them personally. Your time has not yet come, Megan. You are going to show me around your famous greenhouses, remember?'

She hesitated, not knowing what to think. How could he talk about work when he must know how her mind, body and soul ached for his touch?

'If you insist,' she said, but any attempt at dignity was completely foiled by what Gianni did next. His fingers closed on her. Then he slid his hand down her arm until he could grip her hand. He held it for half a heartbeat. In those blissful seconds she was touched by unmistakeable promise, and then released. This was going to be no ordinary meeting between employer and employee.

* * *

Gianni took his time in saying goodnight to his guests. He knew he could afford to. Megan Imsey was *so* hot for him. He wanted to savour the sweet anticipation of her supple little body for as long as possible. As the crowds thinned he began dismissing his staff. Finally, when the night shift moved in to clear away the remains of the dinner, Gianni strolled over to one of the refreshment tables. There he poured two espressos. Meg had been shadowing him closer by the minute. Turning, he held one cup of coffee out to her. The look on her face told him all he wanted to know. Sleeping with her was simply a matter of time. It was entirely up to him when, where and how. That feeling of power was unbeatable. His body hardened with delight, and he smiled. Megan was a smart girl. He had absolutely no doubt she would agree to his terms. He foresaw no trouble at all. Hadn't she told him on her first day that she was only interested in getting paid? That direct approach deserved respect, of a sort. Gianni knew exactly where he stood with women like that. His mother had been a good teacher in that way.

Meg would be all over him from the moment he made his move. Women always were, but the divine Miss Imsey represented something a little different. He watched her concentrating on her tiny cup of coffee. If he hadn't been so practised in the art of seduction he would have thought she was shy. Instead, he identified only the sly upward glances of an experienced seductress, and sighed. Women never gave him a moment's peace. The only respite he'd ever had in the presence of a beautiful woman was Meg's excitement when she talked about those blasted greenhouses. She was as bad as his father had been in that respect. Gianni felt many emotions when thinking about his late father, but pity was the only one he could put into words. He had spent too much time trying to avoid his father's fate to feel anything more. He played the field, determined never to risk falling in love with a woman. Love had driven the old count to live the life of a virtual recluse for nearly thirty years. No way was Gianni going to allow himself to be bewitched like that.

He reached out and pulled an alpine strawberry from one of the floral decorations lined along the refreshment table. A tiny bud hung against the rosy cheek of the ripe fruit. Its stem was as fine as embroidery thread. Scrutinising it with the air of an expert, he saw a perfect flower in miniature, severed from its parent too early. It would never get the chance to flourish and fulfil its promise now. He held it out to Meg.

She shook her head. 'There weren't many ripe fruits available—you have it.'

'No. I've had my fill of perfection. This strawberry may taste as good as it looks, but that isn't always the way,' he said at last, thinking back over his life. 'It's yours.'

He raised the berry to Meg's lips. Obediently, she bit into it. The effect was magical. It was softly, sweetly, fragrant, and everything a strawberry should be. She sighed.

'I can't believe anything could be better than that.'

Gianni felt seduction warming his smile. Unwilling to betray everything that was going through his mind, he soon put a stop to it.

'Oh, no? But I have a second treat in store for you, *cara*. Don't say you've forgotten?'

Everything about his voice told her he was no longer talking about fruit. In a visible agony of anticipation, Meg waited. Gianni began to stroll away, throwing her a few words over his shoulder.

'Come on, Eve. Let's go and find your Garden of Eden.'

The gardens around the Villa Castelfino were a magical place at night. Lanterns fuelled with perfumed wax had been hung from every tree. In their soft light the flowers Meg tended so carefully took on an ethereal quality. Airy canopies of verbena and tobacco plants shimmered in the gloom. As Gianni led her into the new greenhouse complex their shadows danced in the light cast by thousands of fairy lights threaded through the plants. Without realising what she was doing, Meg pressed a button to override the ventilation system and put on some more air.

'I didn't bring you out here to work,' Gianni said severely. 'My father's plans showed fully automatic systems throughout this entire crystal palace.'

'In my opinion there's no substitute for the human touch.'

She spoke without thinking, and instantly wondered if he would pick up on her words. When he said nothing, she began talking quickly to fill the silence. 'What do you think of your father's memorial? You need the proper greenhouse lighting to appreciate the plants. I'll switch it on, and turn these coloured ones off—'

'No—stop. The effect is perfect for what I have to say, Megan.'

She was already walking on into the first bay of the greenhouse. Gianni followed her. She stopped. He came to a halt only when he was close enough for his breath to ruffle the crown of her head.

'I have a proposition to put to you,' he added softly.

Meg whirled around. He smiled down at her in a way

that answered all the questions she would never be able to ask.

'What sort of proposition?' Meg said when she could manage to speak.

'The very best sort.' Tearing his gaze from her, he cast a critical look around the high, airy structure of the greenhouse. Meg's design was so perfect it looked like a tropical glade. Branches hung with orchids and bromeliads rose from a soft mossy bed studded with tiny bright flowers in every shade of amber, ruby and rose opal. The sound of water trickling over a rock face into a shallow pool completed the lush effect. Locked in behind the safety of the kitchen garden walls, Meg and Gianni were alone in her idea of paradise.

'Are you as hot as I am?' He passed one hand over his brow, his breath escaping in a hiss. Meg couldn't bear to think of dark patches ruining the effect of her new designer dress. Slipping off her jacket, she laid it over the nearest branch.

'Before the banquet you tried to tell me you were nervous, but now you're stripping off!' he teased her gently. 'Don't say my delicate little English Rose is turning into a man eater!'

'Lovely as this is, it's still my place of work,' she said with uncomfortable, shy embarrassment. 'I feel overdressed.'

'So do I. May I take off my jacket, too?'

'Of course.'

Once he had removed it, he released the knot of his tie and let it fall loose.

'I can't apologise enough for the way Signora Ricci treated you tonight, Megan. It was unforgivable, even though she has good reason to be bitter. She wants me,' he explained without a flicker of embarrassment.

Every woman must want you, Meg thought, *especially me…*

'I could see that by the way she spent all evening eyeing you up,' she told him. 'I could also see she didn't think much of me.'

'That's why I want to make it up to you, Megan. You're already my ideal employee, hard-working, discreet, and with perfect manners. You put on such a spectacular display tonight, both with your flowers and with the way you coped under pressure. I'd like to offer you an enhanced position, shall we say?' His words were serious, but his beautiful eyes were laughing. 'The fact is, I'd like you to take on a much more hands-on role in my household, *carissima…*'

His final word was a caress as intimate as his touch. He laid his hands lightly on her silk-clad shoulders. When she didn't move, he allowed the tip of one finger to stray beneath the material of her sleeveless dress.

'I'm still not quite sure what you're saying…' she ventured, and then tried to make a nervous joke out of the situation. 'I mean, it's not as though you're about to pull out an engagement ring, is it?' As she looked up at him her gaze was steady, totally unlike the unruly thunder of her heart.

'Of course not—but you're on the right track. You must know what I'm about to propose?' Gianni looked at her closely. Beneath the dozens of tiny coloured lights his eyes were as bright as polished jet, but they dimmed as he realised she had no idea what he was talking about. 'So…you're telling me you have no idea what's on offer?' he said slowly.

Meg shook her head. Watching him, it became obvious

that his natural good manners were fighting a losing battle with something wild and untameable. He looked up and down the shadowy greenhouse. As he did so he rolled his lower lip over his bottom teeth, holding back some remark. Meg watched him suffer until she couldn't stand it any longer.

'What is it, Gianni?' she asked softly.

'I want you to be perfectly clear what I have in mind for you, Megan. It isn't marriage. That is an entirely different contract. And don't even *think* about love. I'm incapable of that.'

Meg's heart began to race so fast she could hear it. She ought to run—hide, do anything but stay with a man who was about to tempt her beyond all endurance. Whatever Gianni said now, she was lost. One way or another, she was about to surrender her whole future to him. She looked up at him in spellbound fascination, not knowing whether to smile or escape while she still could.

He carried on in a low, level voice. 'In my world, marriage is a dry legal process: it's entirely about inheritance and money. It's nothing to do with the way a man needs a woman. It deals only in cold, hard common sense. When I marry, Megan, it will be for the sake of dynasty and ambition. I shall marry an Italian woman who can bring even more wealth and status into the Bellini fold. A man like me finds his pleasures outside that old institution.' His voice dwindled to a whisper. Meg leaned forward, trying to catch his words. Gianni moved in to meet her. His right hand now strayed up to stroke her cheek with a touch as light as thistledown. 'On the other hand, when it comes to choosing a mistress I can afford to look much further afield. And I've chosen you, Megan.'

She had to be dreaming. Gianni's hand idled up to her hair, and then down again, revelling in its silken smoothness. Afraid he might stop if she moved, she stood as still as a statue. Only when he continued his downward exploration, reaching her waist and drawing her in towards his body, did she dare to think it might really be happening. Moulding into the warm, solid power of him felt like the most natural thing in the world.

'You showed me when you first arrived that you're a woman who can stand up for herself,' he went on, 'and I respect that. But if you're going to try and resist me, Megan, I should warn you that no woman has ever succeeded.'

Meg gazed up at him, unblinking. She could believe it. She waited, and then realised he was waiting, too. It was an invitation for her to try and defy his words. She couldn't do it. For long, agonising seconds she floated in the dark depths of Gianni's gaze. They both knew that once the tiny distance between them was breached, there could be no going back.

'There's a first time for everything,' Meg managed eventually. Her voice was nothing more than a breathless whisper.

Gianni lowered his long dark lashes and slowly nodded his head. 'And forbidden fruits taste sweetest,' he reminded her.

She looked up sharply. It sounded as though he had guessed her secret, and with it the real meaning behind her words. The wicked smile dancing around his lips suggested that discovery would make her all the more desirable.

'I want you, Megan,' he whispered.

His honeyed words trickled through her body like warm

water. Her hands gripped his arms. In that instant his mouth clamped over hers. It was firm and possessive, a reassurance that took away all her fears and common sense at the same time. Meg knew this was mad, dangerous and totally wrong, but for once in her life she didn't care. She simply relaxed into his embrace and let his passion engulf her. It was far too wonderful to resist, but she knew she had to make a token effort.

'We can't, Gianni. *I* can't.'

Sliding one hand beneath her chin, he lifted her face. First he placed a kiss on the tip of her nose. Then the need to kiss her properly again overwhelmed him. Meg was powerless to stop him, but when he lifted his lips gently from hers a second time he murmured, 'Of course we can. When I show you how good it can be you'll never want another man.'

'I know…oh, how I know…' Her voice was drifting away with the last of her self-control but there was something he had to know. 'But, Gianni…I can't, really. I don't know how. I've only had one serious relationship, and that ended because he tried to come between me and my work. What I'm trying to say is…I don't know how to love.' She finished in a rush. Gianni froze, and began to pull away from her. When her hands clenched convulsively on his sleeves, he stopped.

'Are you saying you're scared, Megan? That I'm frightening you?'

'No! Nothing could be further from the truth.'

Gianni took her gently in his arms again. This time he cradled her as though she were crafted from finest porcelain.

'Then what is to stop us having the very best of times?

You have no need to worry about love where I'm concerned. I don't know what the word means, either. Certainly, I've never seen it in action.'

She pressed her face against the crisp white warmth of his shirt, desperate to hide her embarrassment. Kissing him felt so right, but in all the wrong ways. She was a virgin, with nothing to offer an experienced man of the world. She wasn't qualified for making love with him once, let alone agreeing to be his mistress! 'This is wonderful, Gianni, but as for taking it any further…I've got no experience…'

'Ah-h-h…' he murmured, his hands beginning a slow dance over the smooth silk of her dress. 'So you're a virgin?'

'It's a bit old-fashioned, I know, but s-sex has never happened for me.' She had difficulty saying the word. 'I was always too busy…I did have a long-term boyfriend, but every time he threatened to come between me and my studies, I backed off,' she whispered into the warm confessional of his arms.

'Then that is what I must do now, *mio dolce*,' he said softly.

That was a shock; it hurt desperately to hear his rejection. 'No! Why?' She looked up at him in anguish.

'You mustn't take a life changing decision in the space of a few seconds,' he warned, but she was determined.

'If only you knew, Gianni. I've waited so long for this experience, and passed up so many opportunities. My focus was always on something else, but now it's my turn to make a decision. I want experience. I want to know what it's like to live as other people do. When I watch you with women, you all seem to be members of some wonderful secret society. I'm sentenced always to be an outsider. I need a taste of real life, Gianni. I've spent years concentrating on my work. Now I want you to be the man who shows me what I've been missing!'

He was quiet for a moment, while his fingertips danced delicately over her back.

'Are you sure?' he said at last.

'I've never been more sure of anything in my life, Gianni. Take me,' she whispered simply.

Outside in the dusk a nightingale poured out its heart in an ecstasy of song. Acting on visceral instinct, Gianni dipped his head and touched his lips to her neck. Meg gasped, revelling in the experience. It was an invitation he couldn't refuse. He wanted to go on enjoying the anticipation of what was to come, but the temptation was too great. Suddenly he was kissing her with more power and passion than she had experienced in her whole life. His tongue urged into her mouth. She let him explore with a relish that had been building since the moment they first met. This felt so right. For the first time in months—years—she was free to put herself first. She had been waiting for so long. Her needs and desires surged in a tumble of excitement. Her hands went up to his head, clawing at his hair to pull him closer. Hungry for his kisses, she was desperate for his attention. His fingertips felt hot through the thin silk of her dress. They circled over her back, ran up and down over her ribs with the sweet certainty of possession. Meg undulated beneath him until the soft pale skin of her inner thigh was rubbing against his leg. It brought back all the turmoil his caresses had as they danced. Now they could release all that pent up passion in one wild moment. She threw back her head with a gasp.

'Oh, Gianni…' she called out, and he was there to answer her cry.

'Good, isn't it?' he purred. The low resonance of his voice was so delicious she could almost taste him.

'Don't stop…please, don't stop…'

'Don't worry, *mio tesoro*, I'm not going to…' His hands roamed over her willing body. His kisses worked their way up from her cleavage and over her neck.

'And now…to make sure you really are as eager as you say, undress me.' The words were growled into her hair. Tentatively, Meg's hands went to the tiny pearl buttons of his shirt. As it fell open, the warm fragrance of his body tantalised her into diving her hands inside, encircling his waist with her hands. Leaning her head against his chest, she pressed her cheek against the soft fur covering it. For longer than either of them realised they clung together in the dappled darkness. Then Gianni's hands stroked her dress up until he could reach the hem. From there he peeled it off over her head in one fluid movement. With it went her last inhibition. She stood before him proudly wearing nothing more than a few scraps of silk and lace.

He smiled.

'You are lovely,' he breathed.

Meg closed her mind to thoughts of how many other women he had spoken to like this. Tonight, he was hers. None of his yesterdays mattered. She could only focus on this moment, suspended in time among bowers of tropical luxury. She didn't care about the shadows. For now a thousand tiny coloured lights illuminated her life.

'This is going to be the best ever…' Gianni whispered, in his element. 'You will be totally mine.'

His gaze now went deeper than mere sexual gratification. He had taken plenty of women in his life, but none had given themselves to him so freely and so willingly. He smiled to himself, fuelled by more than a hint of pride. The experiences she shared with him tonight would colour the rest of her life. She would measure any other man against him—

All of a sudden a frown flitted across his face. For some strange reason, he found the idea of Meg in the arms of any other man unthinkable.

'You can never be anything more than a mistress to me, remember,' he reminded her, caressing the sleek beauty of her hair. 'There can be no strings on either side.'

'I can't think of anything more unlikely than a tethered Gianni.' She chuckled, her voice rich with meaning.

Excitement burned in her eyes. His body sprang to life at the sight of it.

'You'd better believe it,' he growled, rising to the challenge.

Teasing her mouth with his lips, he fed her hunger with his own. She wrapped herself around his body, eager for the penetration of his tongue. The questing point thrust into the accepting softness of her mouth, blocking her moans of pleasure. As Gianni kissed her his hands roamed over the back of her head, twining into her thick silky mane of hair. Meg felt a rising pulse throbbing between them. It was him, it was her, it was both of them, melding in a frisson of excitement. Light-headed with arousal, she ground herself against his body in an ecstasy of anticipation. Gianni responded by trailing his touch down around the curve of her shoulder to mould her breasts with his hands. As his thumbs brushed her nipples a tightening low in her belly pulled breath deep into her lungs. She needed him. Reaching down, she returned his caresses by tracing the shape of his maleness through the soft fabric of his clothes.

Taking her hand, he drew her down gently to the soft mossy bed among the flowers. 'This will be like making love in heaven,' he murmured, his voice thick and low as he released her from his embrace. 'And I shall make it heaven for you.'

Dragging off his shirt, he threw it aside. The sudden movement stirred the soft darkness of his curls into a tousle that Meg could not resist. She stretched out her hand to it. Gianni instantly buried his cheek against her palm, covering the inside of her wrist with a flutter of butterfly kisses. Pleasure danced in her eyes as he stripped off the rest of his clothes and she saw his arousal springing from the soft luxuriance of his body hair.

'Now you're the one who is overdressed, *carissima*!' he purred softly. Meg trembled from head to foot. Her fingers stumbled to help him, but he stopped her. 'No—this pleasure will be mine.'

With a teasing smile, he slid his strong brown fingers between her skin and the thin straps of her bra. Pulling them down over her shoulders, he exposed the glory of her breasts. Meg blossomed under his appreciative gaze. When he closed in on her lips again she moved forward, eager for his touch. As his fingers strayed down to the waistband of her panties she gasped. With infinite gentleness he traced the lace around her waist and over her hips. When his fingers finally insinuated themselves between the wisp of fabric and her skin, she gasped again. A throb of excitement was building up between her thighs. With a moan she felt him ease her panties down, leaving her naked before him.

'And now the teasing has to stop…'

Every inch of her skin was alight with desire for him.

Liquid longing spilled from her body as his fingers spread over her flanks and swept around to caress the sweet soft cleft of her sex. Meg's breath locked in her chest. Driven by an instinct so basic she barely realised what she was doing, she reached out to encircle his erection. Hand over hand she caressed him until he shuddered with a life force as irresistible as her own.

'Not yet,' he growled, pulling her hands away. She moulded her body against his, half delirious with desire. In reply he pressed the length of his body to her nakedness and she gasped in a tumult of longing.

'You must be quite sure—there can be no regrets,' he warned.

'No. As long as this is what you want, too, Gianni.'

He drew back a little, the usual teasing amusement dancing in his eyes.

'Can't you tell? Perhaps I should be asking you the same question!' His touch danced over her erect nipples. 'Although the reactions of your body tell me all I need to know…'

She cried out with pleasure as his fingers swooped down to slide along the crease of her femininity. A million stars exploded over her delicate rose-pink flesh as he sought her clitoris and rolled its tiny bead beneath his fingers with expert delicacy. Her body rose to meet him, pressing upwards against his touch. She was trapped in the promise of his eyes. With tigerish concentration he drew his hand up and over her belly again, resting it there as his other hand drew her face towards his for another long, lingering kiss. She wriggled still closer to him, so eager for the touch of his body against every inch of her skin. He drew shudders of pleasure from her again and again as his kisses traced a line over her throat and across the creamy softness of her breasts. Desire bubbled in her throat and powered through her veins until she felt weak with longing. As his tongue rolled over her nipple, teasing it to a peak of perfection, she locked her fingers in his hair and cradled his head closer to her breasts. The warm glide of his hand swam over her body and she felt her legs part, enticing him further. The dense, soft curls hiding her sex nestled beneath his hand, filling it with warmth. She had known desire before, but never like this. No temptation had brought her to such heights, submerging everything beneath her naked desires. Gianni's thumb nuzzled against the point of her clitoris again and she cried out with longing. His eyes were alight with a fire that burned as brightly as her passion. Mewing wordless arousal, she vibrated with the touch of his fingers. She was desperate with need. It sent her rolling over the bed of flowers with wild abandon.

Gianni was on fire. Meg was unlike any other woman he had ever known. She was so pure, and yet he could inspire all these feral reactions in her. It made her perfect in his eyes, and beneath his body, too. His finger sought out the tender tip of her femininity, circling it until she glistened with pleasure.

'I need to see you—every part of you...' he said thickly, lifting her thighs to rest on his shoulders. As the roughness of his stubble grazed her thin skin he tasted her arousal. It was indescribably good. He had to experience her with all his senses, her rich perfume powering him to still greater heights. He bent his head, running the tip of his tongue the whole length of her swollen creases. Plump with desire, her body spread eagerly beneath his touch. Impassioned cries tore from her throat as she begged and pleaded with him to bring her to a climax. The desire to penetrate her overwhelmed him in a rush of male need. Easing his finger into her, he felt spasms of pleasure grip him again and again. His whole body reverberated with the thought that soon, very soon, she would seize the most sensitive part of his body with the same powerful movements. His heart went into overdrive and a slick of sweat broke out all over his body but he wanted to take his time. Drawing his long, lean finger back even as she clenched down on him, he insinuated a second finger into her willing body. Never had a woman responded to him so eagerly. Her hips thrust against his penetration in a rhythmic dance he longed to complete. Squealing with excitement, she arched her body, working her way beneath him as he pulled her closer. His muscles throbbed with the pressure of restraint as he forced himself to go slowly, extending the pleasure for them both. As the proud swell of his erection finally sought out her yielding warmth he felt her muscles open around him and then close with the pressure of ultimate pleasure. Suddenly, madly, penetration wasn't enough. He wanted all she could give him and more. She was worthy of everything he could give her. In a wild ecstasy of realisation he filled her with every passion he was capable of experiencing. She responded with a primeval cry of pleasure that excited him beyond endurance. This was it, and as he held her in his arms he knew she realised it too.

CHAPTER SEVEN

IN THAT moment, Gianni's life began again. He was used to having the world. Now, with Meg as his mistress, nothing in the universe was out of his reach. The lovely little virgin he had lusted after was now his mistress. The responsibility gave him satisfaction as welcome as his physical release. The moment she went limp in his arms, he picked her up and carried her back through the garden. Taking her through the silent, watchful villa, he laid her gently in his own bed. There they entwined again and again until dawn coloured the skies.

Meg became his consuming interest. No woman had cast such a spell over him before. Her body was sheer magic. From then on, he made love to her at every opportunity. He took her into his bed each night, although it meant he got virtually no sleep. Even when she slept he woke a dozen times a night, simply for the pleasure of reaching out and touching her as she lay beside him. When the praise and orders flowed in after his magnificent banquet, Gianni let his army of personal assistants deal with everything. For the first time in his working life, routine was forgotten. Nothing was allowed to get between Gianni and his ultimate pleasure.

* * *

One morning they were lying in bed together, entwined in the warm afterglow of lovemaking. Gianni's fingers were describing lazy circles on Meg's shoulder as she gazed across to the open French doors. The warming dawn air gently moved the white gauzes draped on either side, giving tantalising glimpses of the blue, misty hillside beyond. The twitter of swallows clustering on sagging, swinging power lines was the only sound in the dreamy warmth of his arms. Meg sighed.

'What's the matter, *tesoro*?'

'Nothing, really… I was only thinking that what you've told me about your life makes you sound like one of those birds. They're always on the move. Until I came here to the Villa Castelfino I'd never been outside of England. My feet were always firmly rooted in my home patch, either waiting for the first swallow to arrive in spring or watching them all getting ready to leave in autumn, like they are today.'

Gianni stopped stroking her. Raising his head, he looked at her quizzically. 'You mean to tell me that my new International Co-ordinator of Horticulture hasn't been anywhere more exotic than Tuscany?'

Meg shook her head. With a smile of perfect bliss she closed her eyes and wrapped her arms more tightly around the expanse of his chest. 'I don't need to, either. I've got everything I want, right here.'

'Yes…'

Gianni sounded thoughtful. Meg opened her eyes. That single word had a worrying note of qualification about it. From the first heady moment of his kiss, her mind had spun fantasies, possibilities and now the fantastic reality of being his mistress. But Meg was painfully aware that her position came with a rigid sell-by date. No matter how lost in luxury she might be, she could not afford to miss the signs that her time was running out. Walking the line between delight and disaster made her sensitive to his every mood.

'That is…for as long as this arrangement suits us both,' she said, careful to sound as unsentimental as Gianni always did. 'I get to network with your international clientele and show off my skills to them—'

'While I get you,' he said succinctly, delivering a loud kiss to the top of her head.

Meg smiled—almost. She had noticed that Gianni was only spontaneous when she couldn't see his expression. He was always more passionate in darkness than in daylight. When, as now, her face was pressed against his chest she had to rely on the vibration of his diaphragm to discover when he was laughing silently. She raised her head quickly, but he was an expert in hiding his feelings. His face showed nothing but the warm satisfaction that had become his trademark since their first night among the tropical flowers.

'Were you laughing at me?'

'Never,' he said in a way that did not convince her for a second. 'Although you must admit, *mio dolce*, an expert on tropical plants—no matter *how* well qualified—who has done all her learning from textbooks ought to spread her wings before she can call herself truly experienced…' he stretched out the syllables with a relish that didn't need explaining. As he smoothed away her frown with kisses she couldn't help smiling despite her private fears.

Outside a hawk streaked into the flock of swallows, sending them screaming in all directions. Meg started at the noise, but Gianni's hand gently stroked away her fears.

'That was why I was going to take you away from all this for a while. Madeira has everything we need. Luxury and opportunities, all set in a sea of flowers. What do you say?'

A paradise island, with the chance to have Gianni all to herself for a while without the daily distraction of his work? There was only one thing she could say. Tipping back her head, she gave him a long, lingering kiss before murmuring:

'That's fantastic. When do we leave?'

Her delight lasted only a few hours. While Gianni was in the shower she borrowed his laptop, ready to surf the Internet. The first page she opened on Madeira fluttered with a banner announcing it to be 'the perfect honeymoon isle'. That headline meant only one thing to her—disaster. She slumped back in her seat, staring at the screen. With an advertising line like that, the place was sure to be full of couples. *Married* couples. That would be the last thing he would want to see. Closing down the computer, she walked slowly across the bedroom, towards the en suite. Gianni was in the wet room. Instead of slipping into the shower with him, she paused outside, deep in thought. It was only when he turned off the monsoon downpour they both loved so much that he realised she was watching him. He chuckled. The sound was low with testosterone. It fuelled her own arousal as he murmured, 'Can't you wait, pretty one?'

Stepping forward, he took her in his arms. Pressing his wet body against her filmy, sheer negligee, he soaked her in seconds. Feeling his manhood spring impressively to life against the smooth plane of her belly, Meg wavered. It would be so easy, so lovely to suspend real life and let him carry her off to bed again, but she felt bound to question him first.

'Gianni…have you ever been to Madeira?' she asked between kisses.

'Mmm…loads of times,' he muttered through the filter of her hair.

'And you like it there?'

'Mmm.' His reply was indistinct, but his caresses were full of meaning. She melted as he lifted her into his arms. 'You'll be perfectly at home, *tesoro*. For you it will be like living in a greenhouse, complete with warm, English-style rain.'

'There's nothing about the place that…worries you at all?' she pressed on, thinking of all those legally happy couples. Gianni was concentrating on carrying her carefully back to his bed.

'No. Not at all. If rain stops play outdoors, then we'll simply have to find some way to enjoy ourselves indoors…'

For a long, leisurely time he showed her exactly what he meant. Meg soon forgot all her misgivings, and surrendered totally to the luxury of his caresses. When eventually she fell asleep in his arms, she was the happiest woman in the world.

Waking later to hear the movement of staff in the dining room beyond his bedroom, Meg reached out for him—and found herself alone. Hearing voices in the main body of the suite, she padded barefoot to the bedroom door. An empty breakfast trolley was being wheeled away, out into the upstairs hall. Gianni was on the far side of the room, his back to the door. Silhouetted on the sunlit balcony, he was chuckling into his mobile phone.

'As I'm quite sure she'll tell you herself—she graduated top of her intake,' Meg heard him telling someone on the other end of the line.

'There's no stopping her. Yet look at me—I've never taken an exam in my life. It's never done me any harm. My father's obsession with these things has led to all this. He's to blame. Yes, I know, I know! Unbelievable, isn't it?'

She could hardly believe it—hardly bear to believe it. Gianni was laughing at her. Worse, he was laughing at her qualifications, behind her back, with a stranger.

Fury surged along Meg's veins with all the power of a tidal wave. From their first kiss she had been bracing herself, ready to lose Gianni to another woman. This was a totally unexpected betrayal. He didn't respect her career. He was humouring her over her work.

That was it. This was the end.

Meg stormed out to confront him. Hearing a disturbance, he swung around, smiling broadly.

'Ah—*scusi*, Chico, something's come up…something very important…' he purred meaningfully, rippling an appreciative gaze all the way up Meg's body as she advanced—until he reached her face. When her expression registered with him he stopped smiling.

'*Ciao.*' Barking the single word into his phone, he snapped it shut and threw it aside. '*Cara mia*—what is it? What's the trouble?'

'You are! I heard you, patronising me!' Meg blazed.

'When?'

'On the phone—just then!'

'Oh, *that.*' He smiled easily, shrugging it off. He moved to take her in his arms, but Meg was having none of it. She backed off. Rigid with rage, she clenched her fists in impotent fury.

'How *dare* you dismiss my work like that?'

Gianni had no intention of arguing with her. He began moving back towards the balcony. 'My staff have set up a table out here. Come and have breakfast in the sunshine.'

His conciliatory tone only enraged her further.

'Don't change the subject! I'm responsible for everything that's been achieved in the kitchen garden since I arrived. Do you always speak to other people about my job as though it's nothing?'

His eyes became points of laser light. 'You're the one who's so quick to say it isn't work to you. I was only repeating what you have said yourself, so often in the past.'

Meg tried to take a couple of deep, steadying breaths. It was no good. Her words, when they came, shuddered with suppressed anger.

'I didn't spend all those years at college for nothing.'

'No, as you're always so keen to remind me you did it to gain a clutch of qualifications and a string of letters after your name,' he responded evenly.

'They got me this job!'

Gianni's expression was unforgiving as he shook his head. 'No, you got this job because you impressed my father. You knew what you were talking about. You had a clear vision of what could be achieved. That was the only thing that secured you this job, Megan. You could have been as under-qualified as I am. We share the same objective, you and I. It's to see the Castelfino estate become as productive and cost-effective as possible. I wanted to do it by expanding the wine business. You came at it from a different angle. I hadn't thought of developing the amenity and visitor side of things until you started the job of restyling the gardens here. A job, I would remind you, that should have died with my father and would have done, if it wasn't for me indulging you to begin with.'

'So you admit it!' she raged. 'You've got no respect for me at all! You're humouring me, every minute of every day! I'm your trophy mistress in the bedroom, then let out to play in your toy garden. It's all for show, isn't it? The moment it suits you to get a wife, I'll be nothing more than one of your outdoor staff again—and an expensive, un-wanted one at that!'

She shoved past him blindly and started snatching up her clothes and shoes from where they had been discarded during their lovemaking of the night before. Gianni held up his hands, trying to calm her as she dressed in a fury.

'You need to calm down, Megan. We both need to take some time out before we say something we regret. I'll run us a bath, and light some of your special rose and lavender candles—'

'Don't bother. You won't get the chance to sweet talk me back into your bed, Gianni. This is it. I'm leaving!'

He stared at her, incredulous. 'You want to leave the Villa Castelfino, and all we have?'

As she dashed past, heading for the door, his hand shot out and grabbed her by the arm.

'Then you're mad.'

She pulled herself out of his grasp, desperate to escape. She wanted to get away from him before her memories of this glorious time together could seep in and change her mind.

'What *is* your problem, *donna*?'

Flinging himself away from her with a curse, he began pacing the room, glaring at her. His fury wasn't a thing to be roused lightly. The desperate need to make a clean break for the sake of her sanity pushed her into a confession.

'My problem is the same as it's always been!' she announced defiantly. 'I came here to work, and not to become your mistress. I don't want to be a second-rank player in the di Castelfino historical pageant!'

'I don't understand. What could be better than life here with me, with money no object?' Gianni hunched his shoulders. 'Women! They're all the same! When it comes down to it, none of you are any better than *her*!'

He stabbed a finger in the direction of a life-sized portrait hanging on one wall of his suite. It was a picture of Gianni's father as a young man, standing beside the most beautiful woman Meg had ever seen. She combined Gianni's come-to-bed eyes and a raven tumble of hair. Her voluptuous figure sparkled beneath a waterfall of gold and diamonds. 'Draped in Dior, weighed down with the priceless Bellini hoard, pregnant with me...yet it *still* wasn't enough for her! My father gave her everything any woman could want, and more besides. In return she made a fool of him, drove him mad, broke his health and his spirit— so why the hell did I think *you'd* be any different? Go on, tell me! What more could you possibly want from me, Megan Imsey?'

Meg felt a pulse throbbing in her head. 'The only things you will never give me,' she said quietly. 'And that's respect. Respect and commitment.'

'Oh, for goodness' sake! This is the twenty-first century, woman!' Gianni threw himself away from the confrontation again. Standing before the great windows of his suite, he seethed visibly. 'Women want it all. With me, they are certain to get it. You've got my body, whenever and wher-

ever you want it. Nothing else was ever on offer. I made
that clear to you, right from the start. What's so wrong with
the arrangement? You're a seasoned businesswoman, Meg.
You must be able to see you're throwing away a better life
than you could hope for anywhere else in the world. As my
mistress, I can give you everything. Believe me.'

No, not everything! she cried out silently, her heart
breaking. *I want you to stay exactly as you are, while
becoming the one thing you will never agree to be—mine,
and mine alone!*

That thought tore words from her like thorns. 'There's
more to life than having a good time, Gianni!'

'Good times like those we share?' Realising anger
would not change her mind, Gianni let his voice become
a low, slow river of regret. Instead of pacing, he now ap-
proached her obliquely. 'I don't think so, and neither do
you, in your heart of hearts. You are my mistress, Meg.
That's been a prize many women have wanted. Grab this
chance of happiness while you can!'

'No…no…I need security. I'm not like you—I can't
afford to think only of myself,' she said, trembling with the
effort of keeping her voice steady. 'Others depend on me,
back at home. I can't let them down, Gianni. They're proud
of me, and the way I've worked. You aren't—no, don't try
and laugh it off. I heard you talking to your friend as though
my work was nothing more than a hobby to keep me
occupied when I'm not warming your bed. I can't stay
here, knowing you think like that. I'll lose all my self
respect.'

Her glance slid away from him in a multitude of emotions. After a pause, Gianni looped one arm around her
shoulders and gave her a reassuring squeeze. It was too

much. Rigid with anger, she burst into tears of rage and shame.

Gianni softened his tone to a seductive purr. 'No, that's not so. We work well together, Meg. Our aims and methods complement each other. They fit together like pieces in a jigsaw. I'll do everything in my power to keep you happy, and keep you here. Name your price—anything. I don't want to lose you.' His hands went to her shoulders and he gave her a tiny shake to emphasise his words. There was no doubting the earnestness in his eyes. It was such a shock to Meg she mastered her tears and stared at him.

'You don't?'

'Of course not! You're the best employee the Castelfino Estate has ever had.' Her spirits rose again. The elation lasted only as long as it took him to add smugly: 'And you come with so very many benefits, *tesoro*!'

She froze, growing up and out from beneath his protective hands. 'Star employee and stellar mistress, in that order?'

'That rather depends…' he said with a lascivious smile. When she still did not nestle into him as she should have done, he encouraged her with a tug. Then he delivered a kiss to the top of her head.

'I don't want to lose you,' he repeated gently.

'In which capacity?' Her reply was clipped and dangerously businesslike.

'Now let me think…'

His fingers trailed over her cheek and down her neck, insinuating their way casually between the neckline of her negligee and her skin. With equal offhandedness Meg moved slightly, away from him and the shelter of his arm.

'While you're thinking, Gianni, I'm going to get

dressed. Then I'm off to tell everyone of my decision to leave.' Her voice was cool and strangely emotionless.

He let her go, instantly on the alert. 'What's your hurry?'

'Because, Gianni, if I stay here, you'll keep trying to change my mind. I don't want that. I want witnesses to the fact I'm going, and as soon as possible.'

'Oh, you know me so well!' He laughed.

In that instant Meg knew there could be no going back. She had touched him for the final time, and could never allow herself to get this close to him again. If she once let him back inside her defences, she would be lost for ever. She could not afford to let that happen.

'Goodbye, Gianni,' she said, her hand already on the handle of the door.

He crossed the room in two strides. Pushing his palm against it, he stopped her opening it.

'No. You must stay.'

Something snapped inside Meg. How could he drag out her torture like this? He was no better than a cat with a mouse, giving her hope then snatching it away again.

'I'm doing this for your own good, Gianni.'

His laughter rumbled around the room. 'Don't be so old-fashioned, *tesoro*! And I hope you aren't expecting life back home with your parents to be the same as before. You're always telling me their sales are increasing by the day. Their success must mean they're still following the business plan you drew up for them. But they don't need you on the spot any more. Stay here with me, Meg. Things will have changed back in England. Your parents are grown people who managed without you, before you were born. They will resent having to make room for you again when they thought you had made a new life here!'

His shocking announcement overshadowed Meg's dread of parting from him. She stared at him in horror.

'How can you say that?' Her voice was a whisper of ice. 'It's no wonder you were so keen to act the playboy if you think parenting is something that ends when children can fend for themselves! Hearing that would have made your poor father despair for his descendants.'

'Leave my father out of this!' he snapped. 'He's got nothing to do with it. His only interest in me was whether or not I would find a reliable, loyal wife. One who was the complete opposite of the woman he chose for himself. But in my experience all women are out for what they can get.'

His last words were a bitter announcement of defiance. Once upon a time his tone would have frightened Meg, but not any longer. She shook her head slowly.

'Then I feel sorry for you, Gianni. It's no wonder you're so dead set against making any sort of commitment to a woman. You must have been damaged in some way, a long time ago.' She gazed at him, desperately trying to strengthen her conviction that she would be better off without the uncertainty of life with him.

His voice was full of the bitterness of unripe olives as he shot a poisonous stare at the family portrait. 'My upbringing took away any capacity I might have had to love, and be loved in return.'

He was quite deliberately twisting the knife in her conscience. 'I'm going, Gianni,' she said, almost managing to keep the tremor from her voice.

'Then you're making a big mistake.'

She hardened her heart and put her hand to the door handle. 'So you say—but I'd rather be free to make my own mistakes in the real world, than locked in a barren paradise like this.'

'Megan—Meg…'

The regret in his voice was so alien, she had to see if it was genuine. Looking at him was almost her downfall. Something glimmered in his eyes just long enough for her to identify it as anguish. Then he stood back from the door with a sigh of exasperation.

'Fine. Go. Do what you like, only never say goodbye to me, Meg.' His eyes were dark with meaning. 'Because between us it can only ever be *au revoir.* We are meant to be together. Apart, we are two halves. Only when together can we be whole.'

'In your mind, maybe,' she said quietly, adding to herself, *but not in your heart…*

'Isn't that the best place?' Leaning negligently against the wall, he watched her open the door. 'That secret refuge where life is as sweet as we can make it, as often as we like?'

Meg put her head down and ran. She headed for her cottage, not caring who saw her. She did not dare stop, because the rip tide of her emotions would drag her straight back into his arms.

'Don't worry, Meg. You'll always have a position here.' His voice followed her out into the upper hall and down the marble staircase. 'You'll be back—and I'll be here. Waiting…'

His chuckle was so delicious. The knowledge she could never afford to hear it again cut Meg to the bone. Squeezing her eyes tight shut against the pain, she refused to weaken, and ran on.

CHAPTER EIGHT

MEG had to keep telling herself she had done the right thing, because it went against every instinct. She knew her spell as Gianni's lover had been doomed from the start. It was bound to end, the moment he found himself a wife. Taking fate into her own hands hadn't made her feel any better. She wrote a resignation letter the moment she got back to the Garden Cottage. As far as she was concerned, it wasn't merely her job but her whole life that was over. Losing Gianni would have been unbearable, until she had heard how little he thought of her. That made it easier—but only slightly.

Though she wanted to leave straight away she was too conscientious to leave her colleagues in the lurch. She did her best to work out her notice without seeing him. It was almost impossible. He had transferred most of his business interests to the office in the villa, so he rarely left the Castelfino estate these days. Until her resignation, he had taken delight in staying at home with Meg rather than roaming the world. If business concerns hadn't started dragging him away again, she would have been in utter despair. Meg knew his future could not possibly lie with her. She prayed he had accepted she would not weaken and tried her best to avoid him whenever she could. Turning aside or hurrying away whenever she heard his footsteps was bad enough. But each time she did it, Meg then tortured herself by watching him secretly until long after he disappeared from sight.

The twelfth of November was to be her last day at work. Meg marked it with a big red circle on every calendar she could find. It sat on the page like a spider waiting to pounce. She tried to see it as the first day of a whole new life. It didn't work. All it signified was the end of her brief, joyous affair with Gianni. That thought made the time pass faster still. And all the time her body was distracting her. She lived in a perpetual state of arousal, needing Gianni, but scared of the consequences. Things came to a head one day when she was cutting flowers for the house. Thoughts of him had kept her awake for half the night. She was tired, and her guard was down. He sauntered up behind her while she was unaware. The first thing Meg knew was the glorious sensation of his hand slipping around her waist.

'Megan—'

'No!' She leapt aside like a gazelle. Avoiding his touch called for drastic action. Thanking her lucky stars that her arms were full of *Monte Cassino* asters, she thrust the airy mass between them quickly.

'What's wrong?' Offended at her reaction, he frowned. It could do nothing to spoil the rising tide of need in her.

'N-nothing. You made me jump, that's all.'

'Does that mean we can be friends again?'

A slow, predatory smile tantalised his lips. He began moving towards her.

'No! I'm sorry—that is…please don't, Gianni…'

Fighting every instinct to throw herself into his arms, Meg shuffled backwards and away from him. For the sake of her peace of mind she could not afford to be seduced by him, ever again. Although he projected the image of an ideal modern man, every fibre of his being was stiff with heritage and aristocracy. The moment Gianni decided the time was right to provide himself with an heir, Meg knew he would see *her* as nothing more than an inconvenience.

'It doesn't have to be like this, Megan,' he said, disappointment clouding his eyes.

'No—thank you. Things have changed. You made it crystal clear how you feel about me and my role here, and in any case it's time I went home to visit my parents. My father is due to go into hospital again soon, so my mum will be glad of company. They need me. Think how you would have felt if you hadn't been able to see your father when he was in hospital!'

She threw out one last desperate excuse, and saw it connect. Instantly the light went out of his expression and he took a step back from her.

'Yes, of course.'

She tried to view her situation through his eyes. From the gossip she had picked up, it was practically standard practice among aristocrats to have affairs among their employees. Gianni had only humoured her over the kitchen garden project because he had wanted to get her into bed. She could see that now. The realisation hurt her more than his anger would have done. That was why she needed to escape back to England as soon as possible.

Autumn blew in with the second week of November. Gianni stood with his back to his desk, hands on hips, watching the sky. It was a wild day. Watercolour clouds billowed over the ridge of di Castelfino land far beyond his window. For centuries his ancestors had watched and waited for attack from the north. Gianni, Count di Castelfino had never feared anything in his life. Now the thought of winter chilled his heart. The bitter wind sweeping down from the Alps wasn't the only thing on his mind.

He strolled back to look at the sheet of notepaper lying open on his desk. Meg's clear, well-rounded handwriting flowed across the page. It was her resignation letter. Reading it again, he almost smiled. Instead of a stiff farewell, she had added thanks for all the help and support she had received, and for the wonderful experience working at the villa had been.

Gianni glanced towards the telephones on his desk, automatically reaching forward. Then he reconsidered, and subsided into his office chair. He was deep in thought.

All his other staff were happy, and none of them had experienced the bonus of his constant physical attention. Why the hell couldn't Meg see when she was well off? He'd offered to do whatever it took to keep her at his side. No inducement worked. Instead she had done her best to disappear off the face of the earth, while still working as hard for the estate as ever. Her influence was everywhere: in the floral art gracing every room of his house, and in the cold empty space beside him in his bed at night.

He had been forced to go around to the kitchen garden several times, trying to find her. He told the staff it was because he needed to make sure she had suitable plans in place for her successor. Not that he had the heart to advertise the post. He already knew Meg was one of a kind. The gardens of the Castelfino estates could sicken and die for all he cared. The greenhouses and flower borders would be too painful a reminder of her, once she was gone. On the few occasions he managed to track her down, she was never alone. She refused to dismiss her staff, and made sure he never got within arm's length. Each time, she went through an emotionless ritual of showing him all the records and computer updates. Gianni couldn't break down the barriers she had raised against him, and he couldn't catch her out on anything. She was impossible to distract. Whether he tried to slip in a sly comment or lifted a quizzical eyebrow expecting a smile, he got the same response. Meg had become a stone-faced company girl to her icy fingertips.

The wind tossed a blizzard of white doves across the autumn-gold slopes of the hillside outside his office window. Gianni barely noticed them. Right now he should be busy on the phone, oiling the wheels of commerce and loving every minute of it. Instead he was wasting time over a letter that took seconds to write and could be binned with equal ease. Snatching it up, he swept Meg's note towards the shredder—but something stopped him dropping it in.

He needed closure. It wasn't something that could be put into words on a featureless white page. There was a need deep inside him to clean out the wound Meg had caused to his pride. It mustn't be allowed to fester. Within twenty-four hours he would be heading across the Atlantic, and the moment would be lost.

He stood up again, roaming around his office like a fury. Not even the display shelves lined with their tasteful objets d'art could distract his attention for long. He lifted a millefiori paperweight, and dragged his finger across the sinuous folds of a modern bronze, but none of these beautiful things made any impression on him. All he could think about was the hole Meg would leave in his life when she left him.

His intercom clicked. He killed it stone dead. Then he dropped his hands onto his desk in exasperation. Meg was wreaking almost as much havoc as his mother had done. But Meg was an intelligent woman. Why couldn't she see that a secure job here with the benefit of his lovemaking was worth a lifetime of scratching a living anywhere else? For the sake of some outdated notion of commitment she would throw it all away and simply because...

He stood up, letting his hands fall to his sides with a smack of infuriation. One minute his life had been running smoothly. The next, Meg had demolished the statue of his pride and left the remains strewn all over the place. It was one thing to accuse him of being incapable of commitment, but to accuse him of being damaged had torn away all his layers of resilience. She hadn't even given him the right of reply. Each time he had cornered her since then, the moment was never right. He always came away with her assurance that everything was under control. That included his reactions. He felt manipulated, without knowing exactly how she was doing it.

The reassurance of her constant presence at his side had been a bittersweet pleasure that had never failed. He frowned, unable to understand how this girl had found something so soft and yielding within him. It was a quality he had never suspected that he possessed. For once in his life, Gianni had stopped looking for his next great conquest.

He wanted the one he hadn't finished with.

Living the perfect modern life with unlimited money

and an intelligent, career-minded woman gave Gianni the best of both worlds. He was in no hurry to relinquish his hold on either.

He set out for the airport next day determined to drive straight there with absolutely no distractions of any kind. He lasted twenty yards. Grabbing the Ferrari's handbrake on with a twang that sent pigeons flying from the trees, he crossed the drive towards the Garden Cottage in a rattle of gravel. No woman had ever walked away from him in the heat of a relationship before. Megan Imsey wasn't going to carve a first on his spirit.

Her little hire car was parked outside. Resisting the temptation to check it for dents, he went straight to the front door. Lifting the heavy black knocker, he dropped it with a bang.

There was no reply. Gianni felt the back of his neck burn with the curiosity of a dozen pairs of eyes, watching secretly from the house and grounds. He didn't care. It didn't matter how many members of his staff saw this. The story would be all around the villa in seconds anyway, whatever he did. That was something else to add to Miss Megan Imsey's list of triumphs.

He was about to lift the knocker again for a second thunderous report when the door jerked right out of his hand. Meg scowled up at him from the doorway. She had one hand cradled in the other.

'You should be on your way to California by now, Gianni.'

Her face was white as paper. It made quite a contrast with the thin red seams of blood running between her fingers.

'You've cut yourself!' He stared down at her, the gyroscope of his anger unable to get a purchase on the slippery slope of circumstance.

'Thank you. I know. I would have had it cleaned by now if I hadn't had to stop and answer the door.'

Meg's crisp defiance was in total contrast with her feelings. The relief at finding Gianni on her doorstep was tempered by the suspicion he was expecting her to faint at his feet like a Victorian heroine. The sight of blood—especially her own—always made her feel wobbly. She felt herself growing into the part of feeble woman by the second, but gritted her teeth. Fainting was most definitely *not* part of her job description.

Gianni clearly agreed with her. Taking charge of the situation, he bundled her into the house and slammed the front door behind him.

'You should be sitting down.' He guided her into the kitchen with a firm hand under her elbow. 'Take a seat while we have another talk about this.' Pulling out her letter of resignation, he brandished it triumphantly.

'Oh, Gianni, I haven't got time for that right now! Look at this mess...' She spread her fingers in a hopeless gesture. Beads of blood were blossoming across the ball of her thumb.

'I'll talk and you can listen while I see to your cut,' he said firmly, grasping her hand and pulling it towards him.

She flinched.

'I'm not going to hurt you.'

'You might. And an argument isn't going to make you feel particularly caring.'

'This cut has got nothing to do with you or me. This is a simple health and safety issue.' He glanced at the scatter of plant material arranged over her worktops. 'What have you been doing?'

'I wanted to take home some mementoes of my stay here. I was preparing some cuttings when the knife slipped.'

He picked her penknife up from the kitchen counter and tested the blade carefully against his skin.

'When was the last time you sharpened this knife? Really sharp knives are always less dangerous.'

Meg looked away. 'I was trying to be quick.'

'Yes, and look where it's got you.'

'All I wanted was some souvenirs,' she muttered.

Gianni dropped the penknife and stared at her.

'You wouldn't need any souvenirs if you simply agreed to carry on working here. You don't have to go, Megan! How often must I tell you? If I said anything I shouldn't, then I'm sorry. You see? This hell is all of your own making,' he finished triumphantly.

'Your memory is painfully short, Gianni. You didn't want to employ me at all to begin with. Now you want my contract to include being your mistress, without giving me any loyalty when you talk about me to your friends. Or any assurance of how long it will last—and we aren't talking only of my career. I need my future to provide a lot more security than you're offering me, Gianni.'

Her voice rang with the resignation of someone who knew exactly what she was up against. This time Gianni couldn't stare her out. The first-aid box was open on the table, so she pushed it towards him. He dropped his gaze to her hand. She stared at the top of his head as he bent over the cut on her thumb.

'It's been hopeless, trying to dress my right hand with my left,' she said, suddenly glad that he was here and taking control. She felt more faint than she wanted him to know.

'I wonder if you might need a stitch or two in this…'

'What?' Meg roused as though from a dream. She stopped, unable to carry on. He wasn't listening to her, but concentrating on her thumb.

'It'll be fine,' she said, trying to convince herself.

'Are you up to date with your tetanus shots?'

'It's practically inscribed in my job description.'

He cleaned the crime scene with all the skill of a surgeon.

'Are you quite sure you don't want me to run you into town to get this looked at? You're very pale.' He searched her face. Meg looked away.

'Thanks, but I mustn't delay you any longer. It's time you weren't here,' she said with chilling certainty.

'Sit there.' He indicated tersely. Meg did as she was told as he began organising scissors, tape and bandage. She watched him, but neither spoke.

She felt she had drawn a line under their affair and said enough: no more. But to her irritation Gianni couldn't leave it at that. He had a pathological need to have the last word, and to always be in the right. Meg had presented him with a wrinkle in his smoothly ordered life. He couldn't leave it alone. He'd had to visit, expecting her to roll over and pander to him eventually, as everyone else always did. She pursed her lips. How could he call himself forward thinking, while keeping a mistress as all his ancestors would have done? If she gave in to her instincts and threw herself into his arms, she would be right back where she'd started. The clock would be counting down the days until he started clearing the way for a wife and legitimate family to replace her. That would spoil any last illusions she had about him. *I'm not falling in with his plans just to salve his guilty conscience,* she thought. As that thought crossed her mind Meg had a flashback. She was in the greenhouse with Gianni. He had played on the sensuality of his caresses all that evening, and made her wildest fantasy into a dreamlike reality. On that first precious evening he had carved his name deep into her heart.

I want you to be perfectly clear what I have in mind for you, Megan. It isn't marriage.

With those few words he had drawn her into a way of life that could only mean heartbreak. She looked down at him as he bent over her hand. It was all she could do not to dive the fingers of her good hand into the thick darkness of his curls. But that would plunge her straight back into his arms and his bed. Meg moved restlessly in her seat. She only felt truly alive with the touch of his fingers and the bliss of his kisses, but she could never risk leaving herself open to the pain and misery of seeing him marry another woman. She couldn't expose her heart to the sort of damage losing Gianni a second time would inflict.

'I've stopped the bleeding. How does that feel, *mio dolce*?'

'Much better, thanks.'

To her horror, Meg realised she was smiling. She had gone into this with her eyes wide open, yet Gianni had still managed to get the better of her. His seductive skills were irresistible. She knew he could sweep her up on wings of desire and take her to indescribable heights. They always shared something way beyond lust or heat. It had been a melding of two spirits…but one of them had resolutely kept a foot on solid ground at all times. Gianni was too keen on watching his back to give himself to her completely. She knew he would never let himself suffer by being led astray.

She watched him as he finished bandaging her hand. Part of her was praying he would leave straight away. Every other fragment of her body desperately wanted him to stay.

'I'd feel happier if you got it looked at the moment you finish work today.'

'Always the thoughtful employer.' Meg sighed. 'It's going to be some homecoming for me, sporting this.' She raised her bandaged hand, because anything was easier than having to look Gianni in the face. He leaned forward, trying to catch her eye.

'How about some strong, sweet tea for the shock?'

His dark eyes were dancing. Meg felt her heart begin to melt, and had to look away. Once he had filled the kettle and switched it on, he picked up her penknife again.

'A blunt blade is dangerous,' he repeated, picking up the pocket steel she had been in too much of a hurry to use. Working quickly he whetted the knife across each side of the file until it was razor sharp.

'That's very impressive,' she acknowledged. 'Although I hope you realise I could have done it myself.'

'But you didn't, did you?' Gianni cross-examined her with one of his unanswerable looks. 'And that's how accidents happen.'

Meg put a hand to her forehead. She had wanted to get on with the work and so hadn't bothered with breakfast, although hunger wasn't the reason why she was feeling light-headed. She was trying so hard to be adult about the situation, yet Gianni was still patronising her. It was impossible to stomach.

'How are you feeling?'

'I'll be great the minute I know you're safely on your way, Gianni.'

'I'm not going anywhere until you've had something to eat.'

Gianni swung around the kitchen counter and opened the fridge. He didn't intend leaving her before he had the answers to a few questions, either. From the way she did her best to resist the temptation to look at him, he knew their shared memories were as fresh in her mind as they were in his. Gianni was accustomed to women falling at his feet, not avoiding his eyes. He was beginning to get the faint suspicion she might have been using him to fill in the gaps in her work schedule. That was an affront to his machismo. He ought to turn his back on her for ever. Somehow he simply couldn't. He told himself it was nothing more than the sight of this blood-stained and bed-raggled little *bambola*, her eyes as big as saucers in her white face. It didn't work.

This is impossible, Meg thought. Gianni was looking at her as if trying to decide which part to devour first. She glanced away, wondering if he was doing it to spite her or whether his face had a naturally insatiable cast.

'You'll have to go, Gianni. The Napa Valley is a long way away.'

'I know, but they won't dare start the meeting without me.'

Her mouth gave a wry twist. He reacted like lightning.

'What is it?'

'This cut is aching a bit, that's all. It's in such an awkward place, right on the ball of my thumb.'

'Then perhaps you'll take more care next time.' He grunted, flipping open the first-aid box again to find her a couple of paracetamols. Returning to her side with a glass of water and the tablets, he glanced away quickly when she trained a look on him.

'Yes. Of course. Thanks for everything, Gianni.' She took the tablets from him, feeling his palm warm and smooth beneath her fingertips. 'It's the first time I've ever cut myself like this.'

He turned his back on her and made himself busy in her tiny kitchen. While he carved a slice of focaccia with laser-like accuracy, Meg took the paracetamols and drank the water. Moving around the room as though he had done similar things a hundred times, Gianni flipped the bread onto a plate for her, and added some flakes of ham.

'Eat that. You'll need to keep your strength up. You're getting much too thin,' he observed unasked.

Meg took a fork from the table drawer. As Gianni's hand dived in to pull out some cutlery for himself they might have touched if she had not been so quick to withdraw.

'You're staying for breakfast?' The words leapt out before Meg realised they could be open to misinterpretation.

'I can't resist this Castelfino ham,' he said with real relish, before his eyes became pinpoints of accusation again. 'Besides, I want to make sure you're going to eat what I've given you, rather than feeding it straight into your Bokashi bin.'

He took a seat on the wide, low sill of the kitchen window. Silhouetted against the glass, he looked every inch the man of her dreams. Meg looked away quickly. She couldn't afford to be distracted. Gianni was as determined to get his own way as she was, and this sudden concern of his was all part of the softening-up process. Demanding that he get out of her home would only provoke a showdown. Meg felt too morally weak to risk that. So instead she kept the conversation light and insubstantial.

'It will be a relief to get back home to England after all this rich food and easy living,' she joked.

Gianni's brow contracted and his jaw tightened.

'Only the English can turn the good things of life into a disadvantage,' he said in an offhand fashion, watching the scarlet claws of autumnal ivy tap against the window-pane. Time stretched between them, elastic yet brittle. Either one could snap the silence and end everything. Meg waited, listening to her heartbeat but deliberately shutting out what it was trying to tell her.

'Stay...'

When Gianni spoke that single word out loud, it was almost too much to bear.

'I can't...I can't!' Dropping her fork, she scrubbed her hand back and forth across her eyes, distracted. 'I don't want to be your mistress any more, Gianni! I'm so used to being in control—I wouldn't be capable of standing by and watching you marry another woman! That would mean giving up all claim to you!'

'So that's what all this is about!' Chuckling, Gianni went to her side and tried to slip his arm around her shoulders. 'Don't be silly—'

'For the last time, stop patronising me!' she blazed.

Realising he had miscalculated, he reined back.

'I came to the Villa Castelfino to work for you—how can I be expected to do a proper job when I'm distracted by being your mistress? I'm torn between two universes, Gianni! Do you really expect me to be satisfied with life on the extreme edge of your orbit? One day soon you'll have the inner circle of your own little family, and I'll be out in the cold. I'll be nothing more than an occasionally useful bystander! That may be your idea of a fulfilled and happy life, but it's not mine! I don't have to be a bit-player in the family Bellini. From now on, my *own* family will be the only thing I'm interested in!'

'Your parents' firm is going from strength to strength. As I said, *they* don't need you now,' he said with feeling.

'Of course they do. How else will they manage while Dad's in hospital?'

He glowered. 'I'll have my people send someone in to cover for them both. I want you. Stay here. With me.'

'I can't. I must go home. I can't stay here!'

He snorted with derision. 'Back to Mama and Papa? When you've tasted life with me? After this, home life will be nothing but a burden, *tesoro*. Your parents have moved on—why can't you? The restrictions of your old life back in England will drive you insane. You won't be able to take quick shopping trips into Florence whenever you feel like it. You won't be your own boss any more. How is that going to feel, when you've thrown away freedom with me?'

The freedom to have my heart broken every time I see you with your new wife? Meg raged inwardly. Concentrating all her pain into her next words, she tried not to dwell on how true they would be.

'You've got absolutely no idea what my life is going to be like once I walk away from here, Gianni.'

'I can guess what life beyond the walls of my estate will be like for you. I feel supremely qualified to judge everything against the life you might have had here. It will never satisfy you. You've had introductions to all the top landowners in the world, and they've had a chance to see your work. You'll never have such an impressive network of contacts again!'

Meg's face burned, but she wasn't about to back down. 'I'll have something far more important back in England. A real home, and a family that loves and supports me. I can't say the same for this place.'

Gianni's voice was emotionless as he crossed to the door. 'Don't blame me if things aren't quite as exciting with your parents as you remember. You left when you were the driving force behind Imsey's Plant Centre. The business has carried on without you, and has kept on getting better.'

Meg had been trying everything to take her mind off her broken heart. Gianni managed to distract her completely with those few words.

'How do you know? Have your "people" been keeping you informed?' She became a seething mass of indignation. It was made worse by Gianni's outward calm, especially when she saw in his eyes that he was struggling with inner tensions, too.

'In a manner of speaking.' His words were full of meaning. 'How could you think I was like other men, not paying attention when you read to me from your parents' letters, or told me about their phone calls? I heard everything you were telling me. Stop looking back. Start concentrating on the future. Walk away from me now, and you will lose everything. When you arrive back home, believe me, you will find you've become a mermaid in an English village duck pond.'

Meg could hardly believe what she was hearing. Of all the arrogant, high-handed attitudes to take, Gianni's was the most outrageous. Anything less than life as his mistress was clearly second best to him. As far as he was concerned, only he could make something of her. To suggest she might manage to have a life outside his charmed circle was beyond his comprehension. Raising her chin to mirror his own determination, she smiled.

'Then I'll just have to carve myself out a bigger duck pond, won't I?'

Without a word, Gianni turned on his heel and walked straight out of her life.

CHAPTER NINE

MEG stood and watched him go. Only one thing stopped her throwing herself at his feet, begging him not to leave. Pride, pure and simple. Pressing both hands against her face she squeezed her eyes tight shut, willing herself not to scream Gianni's name out loud. He was the only man she would ever love. She couldn't tell him, because he couldn't love her.

She heard his Ferrari roar off down the drive in a squeal of wheels and a scatter of grit. Rushing to the open front door, she was met by a smokescreen of dust. It covered his tracks, but Meg couldn't have seen him anyway. Her eyes were too full of tears. Slamming the cottage door, she ran upstairs and threw herself face down on her lonely single bed. Telling herself a clean break would be the best way was so easy. Experiencing the actual agony of losing him was hell.

She cried until the shadows lengthened. Only the pressing need to pack and escape got her through the next few hours. All the time her hand throbbed against the bandage Gianni had tied. How ironic that the last memento she would have of him was a tight binding. Wild ideas about never taking it off swam in and out of Meg's mind as she tried to cling onto Gianni's memory. All she had was this dressing to remind her. The cut on her thumb might not even carry a scar.

Unlike her heart.

Meg travelled back to England in a daze. She got off the bus outside the local pub and completed the last few hundred yards of her journey on foot. It was time to clear her head and get a grip. She needed to work out some coping strategies—for losing Gianni, and for telling her parents she had thrown away the best job she was ever likely to get. Walking up the lane towards home, she decided work would have to come to her rescue, yet again. She smiled for the first time in days. It was a weak, watery expression, but it was progress. She began to look forward to her mum making a fuss of her. After they had shared a nice pot of tea and some comfort food, Meg would retreat to the greenhouses and immerse herself in the million and one odd jobs that must have piled up since she left.

The once-potholed country lane leading to her old home was now a smooth, well-made road. Meg was too full of her own thoughts to notice. It was only when she rounded the final bend she realised Gianni had been right. Things certainly *had* moved on since she left.

The shock stopped her dead in her tracks. Her hands fell open with surprise and dropped all her luggage on the tarmac with a crash. Imsey's Plant Centre had a whole new entrance and car park where the old sheds had been. A bright yellow mechanical digger was working behind the greenhouses Meg had been so sad to leave. It was burrowing across a field that had once belonged to their neighbour—but no longer. With growing disbelief Meg took in the message printed on a smart board beside the nursery entrance. It apologised to customers for any inconvenience caused during phase one of the nursery's expansion scheme.

Gianni's words came back to haunt her when she reached the plant centre's entrance. Not only was there now a gate, it was locked.

She was shut out of her own home.

Pulling out her mobile, Meg rang her home number. To her horror, a complete stranger answered.

'What's happened? Where's Mrs Imsey?' Terrified, Meg was already hurling her cases over the gate and starting to scramble over.

The voice went stiff with authority.

'I'm afraid Mrs Imsey is unavailable at the moment. May I help you?"

To Meg's intense relief, her mother suddenly appeared in the bungalow doorway and waved. Dropping her phone, Meg ran up the drive, but it was a very different woman who rushed towards her in greeting.

For one thing, Mrs Imsey was wearing a dress. And she only threw a single arm around her daughter to begin with, as she was busy signing off a mobile call herself. It was on a PDA that looked almost as impressive as Gianni's.

'Megan! There's lovely!' Engulfing her daughter in a proper hug, she almost squeezed the life out of Meg—until the unmistakeable strains of Percy Grainger danced from Mrs Imsey's mobile.

'Sorry, lovey, it's the design studio. Can you fend for yourself for a bit? There are some ready meals and chips in the freezer—' Mrs Imsey said, before starting to speak into her phone again.

Meg had no option but to stand and wait until her mother's call was over. She might be in the middle of her parents' drive, but she was all at sea. Except during family celebrations she had never seen her mother wear anything but overalls and wellington boots. Not only was Mrs Imsey now dressed in wool jersey and court shoes, she was using a mobile phone. And one that chirruped 'Country Gardens', too…

Meg knew she should have been glad, but the mention of junk food made her suspicious. Her mother would have considered it unthinkable a few months ago. She was torn between delight and unease. There was no need to wonder what had happened since she had been away. Gianni's words echoed through her mind like a passing bell. Her parents really had moved on. It was Meg who was living in the past now.

'I'll go down to the greenhouses and find Dad,' she mouthed to her mother. Initially, he had been more reluctant than his wife to take Meg's improvements on board. Now Meg couldn't wait to see him again. He would be her anchor in the middle of all these changes.

Her mother waved a frantic finger then covered the mouthpiece on her phone before pointing at the house.

'Your dad's in the office, installing some new software on his laptop. If you want anything special from the supermarket, he's going to be updating the grocery order later, but you'd better be quick!'

Meg gaped. When she'd lived at home, her father had only emerged from his beloved greenhouses at mealtimes and dusk—sometimes not even then. She had tried to get him to use the elderly office computer a hundred times.

Meg suddenly felt an awfully long way behind the

times. Looking at all the hustle and bustle going on around her once sleepy little home, she wondered if her parents had missed her.

Meg moved her things back into her old bedroom, but Gianni was right. It was no longer home to her. Life with him had made her a nomad, unable to retrace her steps. Although the clothes she had left behind in her wardrobe hung loosely on her now, she had grown. Her return felt like trying to fit a Boston Ivy into a three-inch pot. She wanted to escape, but didn't know how. Her parents no longer needed her. She was free to go, but now she was the one holding back. She had a Gianni-shaped hole in her life. Nothing, not even her family and friends, could fill that.

In desperation, she threw herself back into work at the nursery. Learning all the new systems and meeting all the extra members of staff was a refuge. It wasn't enough. She needed Gianni to keep her centred. Without him, her life had no balance. Despite her desperation, she was proud. Scouring the trade press to see if he would advertise the position of International Co-ordinator of Horticulture felt too desperate. So she resorted to inventing a new job for herself. Capitalising on her success at Chelsea earlier in the year, she designed and fitted out a trailer, specifically for transporting their plants to national flower shows. It was nothing more than frantic displacement activity. Concentrating on Imsey's Plant Centre stopped her agonising over the future she had lost…until something began working its way into her consciousness. She had started to feel decidedly strange. Her breasts became tender, and she couldn't remember the last time she had seen a period. That was hardly surprising, when her mind was so full of Gianni—but it was worrying.

She no longer lived each day to the full. All she did was exist. Getting up before dawn and working all day, she did nothing more than go through the motions. She opened up the business each morning, and closed it down last thing at night. When her parents persuaded her that she must have some time off, she spent it in her room. There she wrote up the notes she had made while working on the Castelfino estate. At least, that was what she intended to do. Instead, she sat at the writing desk her parents had bought her for her sixteenth birthday and stared out of the window. She had looked out over these fields and hedgerows all her life. Until today she had always been able to find something new and interesting about the view. The sight of redwings arriving to feast on hawthorn berries usually worked as a reminder to start making her Christmas lists. Today she stared at the cackling flock without seeing anything. Her mind was far away, on the other side of the Alps. Snow would be falling on those mountains, but they could look forward to spring. Meg couldn't. From now on she would be in suspended animation. It was for ever winter in her heart. She had sacrificed everything, and for what?

Stop it, she told herself viciously. *My heart is too full to bear, but it's nobody's fault but my own. I made the decision to cut my losses and run away from Gianni. If it wasn't for my stupid pride I could have stayed, at least for a little while longer. Now I have to live with the consequences of leaving. That means me—not the people I live and work with. They deserve better than the sight of me moping around the place!*

With a huge sigh and an even bigger effort, Meg put her hands flat on the desk to lever herself upright. Outside, life was going on without her. She might be dead to the world, but that didn't mean everyone else had to suffer. Beyond her bubble of grief, the sun was a ball of fire, touching the fields with gold. She stood up, but felt suddenly dizzy. She had to clutch at the desk for a second to steady herself. That was a shock. It was then she remembered she hadn't been able to eat anything more than a few crackers all day, because she had been feeling queasy.

An awful suspicion began to form in her mind. It might be nothing more than a vicious circle of grief killing her appetite, which made her permanently tired and sick at the very thought of food, but on the other hand...

It was ridiculous, of course. She couldn't possibly be pregnant. Gianni had been meticulous about taking precautions.

She couldn't be pregnant.

She couldn't be! She stared at the sunset, trying to think. It was hopeless. There was only one way to ease her mind. Picking up her purse, she headed for town. The pharmacists stayed open later there.

The next few days passed in a blur. If it wasn't for the huge wall planner blocked out in vivid inks and the reminders popping up on the business computer system, Meg would have been incapable of achieving anything. As it was she went through her routine on autopilot, selecting plants, packing the trailer and heading up to London to stage an exhibit of the Imsey Plant Centre's finest flowers. It was a nightmare. The streets were full of pregnant women. Buggies jostled for space on every pavement. Babies were everywhere. Meg had never noticed them before. Now they were all she saw, but only one mattered to her:

Gianni's child, growing inside her. She could think of nothing else. Normally the prospect of building a stand at one of the Royal Horticultural Society's monthly shows would have terrified her. Now it was one more thing to distract her when she had something far more important to worry about. Everyone she saw, wherever she looked, was part of a family. It should have made her glad. Instead her heart became heavier and heavier. The perfect picture of Mum, Dad and children would never be part of her life. She had no room for any man other than Gianni. A single parent could never afford to let their guard drop for an instant. All the responsibility would be hers—caring for her baby, earning the money to keep it fed, clothed and housed…and all the time that little face would remind her of the man she had left behind.

She arrived early at the hall where the winter flower show was to take place. Her mind could never leave Gianni alone, but the work had to be done. Her orchids were in perfect condition, and she wasn't about to sacrifice them. She had been up for most of the night, cushioning each bloom with cotton wool and securing every flower stem. Now all the tape and packing had to be removed. It was a fiddly job, but Meg knew exactly what she was doing. Her fingers flew over the work and soon she was settling each flower pot into the Imsey Plant Centre display. Before long her table had been transformed into a miniature rainforest. As she was congratulating herself that there was still plenty of time before the show opened a shadow fell over her.

Meg's sixth sense instantly told her it was Gianni.

She was right. Whirling around, she looked up into the face she had longed to see, and touch, and kiss for so long.

A million thoughts tangled through her mind, but she was saved from making a fool of herself. Gianni was not alone. He was flanked by a man in a dark coat, and a teenager holding a very expensive looking digital camera.

'*Buon giorno*, Megan. These gentlemen are journalists. They produced a feature for a Sunday supplement on the work we have done together on the Castelfino project—'

'The work *you* did,' she interjected. The men smirked at Gianni. He ignored them, and speared Meg with a glare. He cleared his throat meaningfully.

'I happened to be attending a conference in England, and took care to check their copy while I was here. It was a good thing I did. I don't want a feature aimed at the lucrative Christmas market telling only half the story. They are missing your contribution and some photographs, and they needed *my* influence to get them in here before this place opened,' he said before she could ask why he had bothered to come with them. His words were fired like bullets from a gun. Meg saw straight away that Gianni didn't intend the journalists to get any sort of human interest angle.

'I don't know…' she began faintly. From his stance and the gaze he was directing carefully over the top of her head, this was not the way Gianni wanted to spend his time in London. It looked as though the pain wasn't all on her side. Fighting the urge to throw herself into his arms and beg forgiveness, Meg tried to put herself in his place. He was doing the right thing, despite the way she had treated him. She owed it to him to put on a brave face and toe the company line. So she smiled, and answered all the journalist's questions. After carefully leaving out all references to her stellar qualifications, she was horrified when her interviewer brought the matter up. With a quick side-long glance at Gianni, she glossed over the matter. After what he had said in the past, he wouldn't want reminding about them. The photographer worked as she talked, so the whole horrible process didn't take long.

As her visitors left all Meg's pent up emotion escaped in a low moan of anguish. Despite all the noise and bustle of exhibitors setting up around her display, Gianni heard. He stopped, dismissed the journalists and walked quickly back to the Imsey stand.

'What's the matter, Megan?'

With his companions heading out of the main doors, she expected him to smile. He always smiled when he asked how she was feeling.

But not today.

She swallowed nervously. 'Nothing—I'm fine. That interview was just a bit of a shock, that's all. I'm not used to things like that being sprung on me at a moment's notice. It made me nervous.'

'That was why I stayed with them. In case you needed some moral support,' he said tersely.

She thought of his morals, and her baby. Given the circumstances, Gianni couldn't possibly want this child as much as she did. He wouldn't want it at all. She came to a split-second decision. The less he knew, the less power he could have over her.

'I assumed you were making sure I didn't bad-mouth you to the gentlemen of the press,' she said casually.

His grim mask slipped a little, and he looked shocked. 'No. I know you're far too much of a professional to do that. I also knew you'd be too self-effacing when interviewed. I came along to ensure you got your fair share of the credit.'

'That's all?'

He didn't answer.

'Then thank you, Gianni,' she said quietly. 'When will the article appear?'

'In time for a big promotion I've been arranging in England. That's why I'm over here,' he said, quashing any idea that he had travelled from one side of Europe to the other to win her back. Meg knew then she had made the right decision. She could not possibly let him know about the baby. She would dissolve like meringue at the slightest hint of either his hatred or his pity. She needed him to carry on being the rigid, emotionless aristocrat standing before her.

'Well, as you're here, shall I supply you with another raft of plants for your latest harem?'

The joke almost lodged in her throat, but she got the words out somehow. Managing to smile was quite a different prospect. It was hopeless. Quickly, she busied herself gathering up a few last tufts of cotton wool and compressing them into a tiny ball, the size of her atrophied heart.

'Not quite. I only need one.'

Meg's blood curdled in her veins. There could be only one possible interpretation she could put on his words.

'Only one? Then it didn't take you long to find a replacement mistress.' Her movements were light and careless. They fluttered over the soft moss of the display, refining the tilt of each orchid bloom or broad, smooth leaf.

He shook his head. 'From the way you kept reminding me of all your qualities, I'm surprised you hadn't realised you were irreplaceable, Megan. For your information, I'm no longer in the market for a mistress. Not now, and not ever. That part of my life has come to an end.'

'Then…' She looked at all the plants she had so artfully arranged in her display. They were all in groups. She was the only singleton, now and for ever. 'That must mean you've found yourself a wife.'

'Possibly. The final details still have to be decided.'

Meg looked away so he would not be able to see the pain in her eyes. 'You make it sound like a business proposition.'

'That rather depends on the arrangements reached. This is my last night in London. I'd like you to bring the plant around this evening.' He pulled out his PDA, tapped a few buttons and cross-referenced its display with his wrist-watch. 'I shall be free from seven p.m.'

It sounded chilling. Meg stared at him, knowing this should be the last time they met.

'Will your fiancée be there?' she asked gingerly.

His mouth became a tense line of disapproval at the word.

'I have a window of opportunity at seven. That's all,' he announced. Then he was gone.

CHAPTER TEN

MEG could not bring herself to be petty or mean-minded about the plant she chose to fill Gianni's order. She took her own favourite plant from the display. It had the most beautiful flowers, white petals overlaid with a pink flush and set off with a delicate yellow lip. She took great care in wrapping it. Crackling cellophane would protect it from the December chill, while the yards of pink ribbon she curled to decorate her offering made the finished plant a present she would like to receive herself.

The address of Gianni's Mayfair apartment was engraved on her heart from their first meeting. That didn't prepare her for the reality of it. A uniformed doorman showed her in. A phone call had to be made by Reception to check that she was a legitimate visitor. She was whisked up to a penthouse suite by a lift that was whisper quiet. Stepping out into a world of thick, plush carpet and gently hissing air-conditioning, she was faced with a sleek featureless door. There was no handle, knocker or any suggestion who might be behind it. Meg raised her hand, but she didn't have time to knock. A maid in a smart black uniform and white apron opened the door. She lifted the gift-wrapped orchid from Meg's hands, but was distracted by a movement from inside the flat.

'*Grazie*, Consuelo. You can go home when you've dealt with that,' Gianni's voice murmured out to greet her. Despite everything, Meg's heart leapt. When he moved into her field of vision, it stopped altogether. Instinctively, her hand moved to her waist. Then she let it fall away. Gianni mustn't suspect anything. Tonight, he looked every inch the career bachelor. Moving easily around his spacious apartment, he was in his element. He hadn't changed out of the suit he had worn for his meeting with the journalists, although he had lost his tie and jacket and his feet were bare. He had removed his gold cufflinks too, and his shirt sleeves fell back to expose his beautiful tan.

'There wasn't a chance to thank you for everything you've been to me. I wanted to spend some time catching up with each other,' he said to Meg as the maid pulled on her coat and wished them both a good night.

It sounded a hideous idea to Meg. The last thing she wanted was to be force-fed details of the woman who had overcome Gianni's lifelong aversion to marriage.

'How long do we have?' Meg asked as he led her further into his flat. She looked around with small, nervous movements. Desperate to find any trace of the Other Woman, she was sick with fear she might actually see something. There was nothing obviously feminine on display. Gianni's apartment was a masculine blend of clean lines and expensive furnishings. Silver curtains held back by golden ropes brushed a luxurious white carpet. Beyond the windows that ran the whole length of one wall, London by night was spread out in a kaleidoscope of flickering lights.

'We have as long as *I* like,' Gianni announced. 'I need

to explain something to you, and must be absolutely certain you have it straight in your mind.'

She nodded dumbly. Moving over to a low coffee table made of a single piece of solid beech, he picked up a crystal decanter of cognac. Two glasses stood on a silver tray. Splashing a finger of spirit into each, he offered one to her. Still lost for words, this time Meg shook her head. He shrugged.

'Suit yourself—I'll leave it on the table. You may feel like it later.' Holding his glass up in the soft glow of wall lights scattered around the room, he admired the clear golden liquid before taking a mouthful. It met with his approval, and he smiled. Seeing his face touched by a trace of the pleasure she had seen there so often, Meg smiled, too.

'I was wrong, Meg,' he said unexpectedly, diving in under her guard. 'I thought that to make you anything more than my mistress would turn you into a woman like my mother. She was a wife, and the ruin of my father. I thought committing to you would submerge everything special, unique and priceless about you beneath a tide of greed. Can't you see? I couldn't take the risk of getting emotionally entangled. As my mistress, I could preserve you as my ideal woman, for ever. Marriage would turn you into a wife, and the Meg I knew deserved better than that. You were soft, sweet and sensuous—the ideal mistress, perfect to visit after a hard day at the office. I wanted to keep *you*, not some shrew obsessed with gym membership and spa treatments. Seeing you turned into all the worst memories I had of my mother was the very *last* thing I wanted.'

It was a long speech, delivered as Gianni stared down

into his glass. Meg stirred, wondering what she could say. He hadn't finished. 'My earliest memories are all of conflict. My mother screamed the whole time, my father shouted, and it was all carried on in a windmill of gestures. My childhood was punctuated by the sound of crockery shattering against every surface. I didn't want to live like that. And then you arrived, wanting more than my body, or my money.'

Confused though she was, Meg couldn't let that go.

'I thought you said your mother died in childbirth?' she probed. In the past few moments her face had worked through every emotion. Fear and confusion had passed. She was now tense with suspicion. Her fingers running back and forth softly across her waistband, she waited for his reply.

'A child did cause the death of my mother, but it wasn't me. My half-brother was stillborn.'

Meg couldn't speak. Nothing she could say seemed appropriate. Finally, when Gianni's shoulders moved in a silent sigh, she reached out and placed her hand on his sleeve.

'Your father must have been devastated,' she said softly.

This time there were no explanatory smiles. He shook his head in despair.

'You have no idea.'

He swore, a bitter Italian explosion that he could not stifle. Meg looked away.

'As a child I assumed he was heartbroken. He was—but loss of trust damaged him far more than my mother's death. She'd conducted affair after affair, eventually falling pregnant to one of her many lovers. My father never spoke of it to me at the time, but shut himself away in the Villa Castelfino. I was sent off to school in England. Someone must have thought I'd be protected from the gossip and stories. They didn't count on the cruelty of children. In our isolation, both Papa and I grew shells of steel. The moment I left school I came home, hoping we could be a support to each other. I tried to help, but it was no good. He would never mention it. He encouraged me to go out and enjoy myself, on the absolute understanding that the woman I eventually chose to marry was perfect Bellini family material. Papa spent every moment of his life regretting his choice of wife, and didn't want the same thing to happen to me.'

'What a terrible example of married life.' Meg said slowly, thinking of her own parents' idyllic partnership. 'No wonder you never wanted to be tied down.'

'I wasn't going to let my heart lead me into disaster. My father married for love and was cheated. If my own mother couldn't be faithful, how could I possibly trust any other woman?'

'We aren't all alike.' Meg got her point across firmly. 'It's a good job my mum is nothing like yours. At least she wasn't, before I left for Italy…'

'Things have changed?' He gave her a knowing look. She nodded.

'I told you so,' he said, but with such regret Meg knew he was sympathising, not trying to score points.

'It's nobody's fault, Gianni. I left you because my feelings were hurt. When I got home, I realised you were right. Times change, people move on. I should have been confident enough in my own abilities to shrug off whatever you and your friends thought about my work. I know I would have proved you all wrong in the end. And I should have been big enough to part with you on better terms.' She stopped. There was a lump in her throat that threatened to betray her real feelings. 'We have to end this properly, right now,' she said in a rush.

'Of course.' Gianni's practised ease broke her heart into still smaller fragments. This must be a regular occurrence for him. A tearful girl, the fond farewell, the pretence of regret…

A mobile phone buzzed angrily from somewhere. Putting down his glass, he strode over to where his jacket lay on a chair. Retrieving the handset from an inside pocket of his suit, he muttered a curse and killed the call without answering it.

'That reminds me—you'll have to take my details off your BlackBerry,' Meg said, hoping he would ignore the quaver in her voice.

'I can't,' he said frankly, 'because they were never on there.'

The pain that had tortured Meg for so long swam into her eyes. Working hard to master her features, she managed to look up at him in undiluted defiance.

'But all your vital numbers are stored on there!'

Shocked by her tearful response, Gianni's retort was rapier swift.

'Not yours. Oh, don't look at me like that—what else did you expect? Would you rather I lied to you, and said it was on there? No, thanks. I leave deception to people like my mother.'

'Gianni! How could you be so heartless?' she said bitterly. 'If you ask me, I think you just use your father's experience as an excuse not to marry because you're too selfish! I'll bet in reality he couldn't wait to see you safely married!'

'What?'

Her jibe threw him completely off balance. For long seconds he stared at her, totally unable to summon up enough English to reply.

'While you were stuck in a time warp of commitment-dodging, your father was always more interested in the future. I spoke to him often enough to know the Bellini traditions wore him down. He was ready for change. I think he would have loved to see you married, Gianni. He'd probably got to the stage where he didn't care who she was, as long as she loved you for all the right reasons, and that you'd chosen her for all the wrong ones—such as your raging testosterone.'

'What do you mean by that?' Gianni retorted, but his surge of anger brought more turbulent emotions to the surface. He frowned. 'I was his heir. He *had* to care. When I think of the times he raised his eyebrows over breakfast when I was headline news again…when he asked me why I never brought any of the girls home to meet him, I thought he was being sarcastic. And the celebrity dinner parties he held in New York or Athens where all the guests had daughters…' Gradually his voice faltered. When it disappeared altogether he gazed into the middle distance as though in search of it.

'So that's your defence against marriage blown right out of the water. He wanted you to get moving. Now you've got no excuses left, Gianni. Say goodbye to me now, so you can go and present the orchid I brought you to the poor long-suffering woman who is going to become your wife.'

The mention of excuses brought him straight back to the present. Grabbing her hand, he began to pull her through the lounge. Meg thought he was about to throw her out of his suite altogether, but she was in for a shock. Instead of heading for the main door, he took her into an adjacent dining room. An intimate dinner for two was planned. The central table was set with a battery of silver cutlery and bone-china plates decorated with a discreet pattern in gold leaf. In the centre stood the orchid she had brought, still decked in its cellophane and ribbons. The lights were low, and the room warm and welcoming.

'An aristocratic Italian girl is the last thing *I* want,' he muttered, guiding her around the table. The far wall was almost completely filled by an enormous mirror in a heavy gilded frame. Below it stood a highly polished walnut sideboard. As they got closer Meg saw a young lemon tree in a terracotta pot standing in the centre of the sideboard. Everything glowed and shimmered in the light of dozens of candles.

Gianni looked as distracted as she felt. His tousled hair and open necked shirt gave him a reckless look, but his manner was anything but spontaneous.

'Your resignation was a real wake up call to me. I've spent every second since then examining my motives. I'm still convinced you did the wrong thing, Meg.'

'That doesn't surprise me.'

Before the accusation had fully left her lips Gianni grabbed her by the shoulders.

'Wait! Listen to me—you've driven a hole right through my reasoning, Meg. Do you hear that? All my life I've been working towards what I thought my future should be. I wanted a legitimate son to carry on my family name. That's still my objective, but you've made me realise I was going about it all the wrong way.'

Meg narrowed her eyes. 'How many ways are there to break a woman's heart, exactly?'

He flung his arms wide with exasperation.

'I thought I was being the ideal forward-thinking executive, but in reality I was always looking back over my shoulder. I was surrounded and haunted by the expectation of the past and the duty of being count.'

She watched him carefully, wishing she could read his expression. Gianni had hurt her more than she could bear, but she should have expected that. They weren't simply from different sides of the track, they were from opposite sides of Europe. Aristocrats were one thing. Foreign aristocrats were still more enigmatic. She loved Gianni so much it hurt, and would have done almost anything to take this look off his face. The only thing she could not bear to do was sacrifice her pride by asking how she could help. Meg might be meek, but acting as a doormat was not her style. She shook her head. With that, he indicated the potted lemon tree standing before them.

'And so I came to a decision. *Presto!* What do you think of this?'

From every branch hung a small package wrapped in red velvet. Each one was suspended from fine gold wire and the weight caused the little bush to bow and tremble in the warm air.

'It looks like a Christmas tree,' Meg said slowly.

'They're all for you.'

Hesitantly, she took a step forward. The little presents begged to be touched, taken and opened. Somehow, she couldn't do it. He must be trying to buy her off. In her fevered imagination they represented drops of her heart's blood, and they sprang from loving him. Slowly, she ran her hand over the back of his as he held her by the wrist. She knew every contour as well as her own. This would be the last chance she had to savour that smooth, taut skin. His fingers had to be peeled away from her. She had to release him so that both he and her baby could be free. It tore strips from her heart.

'Go on—they're yours,' he insisted. 'If you want them.'

'They're all for me? Why? I don't want anything more from you, Gianni. Not now.'

He started to say something but she held up her hand and stopped him. 'I never expected to see you again, but since I'm here there's something I really must tell you. I can't possibly keep it a secret. You won't like it, but I can't keep the truth from you—'

'Wait. I have a confession of my own,' he interrupted swiftly. 'It's one I should have made a long time ago, Meg. Let me say it while I can. If only I could have been honest with myself from the start, I could have saved us both so much pain.'

'Gianni…' Light-headed with lack of oxygen, Meg struggled for words but couldn't think straight, much less speak.

'When I first saw you, I was having the time of my life. All the women I wanted, more money than I could spend— I was the original man who had everything. But it was all a sham. All my life I've been fooling myself that happiness could be bought. I was wrong. It has to be earned. When I was a child, I watched my parents tear each other apart. The connection must have been made deep in my mind between marriage, anger and despair. My father tried to do the right thing by conforming to the model our ancestors carved out of ancient history. But after growing up to the sounds of screams and smashed crockery, I headed in exactly the opposite direction.'

'I suppose that's understandable,' Meg said faintly, her

stare unblinking. She couldn't take her eyes off the man who, always such an enigma, was struggling to open up in front of her.

'I used to hear my mother goading my father, right up to the end. She had so many lovers even she couldn't put an end to the press speculation about the identity of my half-brother's father.'

'Oh, Gianni...' Tentatively, Meg reached out towards him. He was staring at the ground as though his eyes could bore right through to the centre of the earth. It made her hesitate, her hand halfway to his shoulder.

'That's why I told myself I'd never get married. I'd seen what it was like, from the inside.' He recoiled with a grimace. 'But, *Dio*, in my book if a man makes love to a virgin, marriage is the only option. I should have made you my wife the very next day. The trouble was...I couldn't face the possibility that marriage would turn us into the sort of monsters I remembered from my own childhood. What if I failed in the one and only thing in life that truly matters—love? And to expose another innocent child to the hell I endured—I couldn't do it. Then again, I wasn't going to lose you. So I carried on with the fiction that you'd always be my mistress but never my wife. Every time I told you that, it was my guilty conscience talking.'

It went very quiet. For endless seconds, they neither moved nor spoke. Tears clawed at Meg's throat, eager for release, but she was determined never to weaken in front of him again. He'd admitted he'd wanted to marry her, but couldn't bring himself to do it. If she mentioned the baby now, he would think she was trying to force his hand. She stood in silent, bitter, lonely darkness until she could stand it no longer.

'Then I'll say goodbye,' she said in a small voice. 'You've unburdened that guilty conscience of yours, so there doesn't seem to be anything more to say.'

'Goodbye? Is that what you truly want, Meg?'

'What do you think?'

For once their roles were reversed. Meg's voice was low with determination. When at last Gianni spoke again he sounded unusually reluctant. 'You said you had something to tell me. I interrupted you, *tesoro*.'

The uncertainty in his voice was so unnatural Meg's eyes flew open.

'Don't call me that. You don't mean it.'

'Yes, I do. Of course I do. I've never meant anything more sincerely in my entire life.'

Meg stared at him. Now she really was confused. Perhaps she was hearing things. She certainly felt feverish enough to imagine his touch—

No, that at least was true. He had extended his hand until it was resting on her arm. His touch was as light as an orchid petal.

'Open your presents, Meg.'

Every ounce of his usual authority filled the order. Meg jumped towards the pretty little decorated tree before she could stop herself, but the second she could, she did.

'Go on. You know you want to.' His voice was slow and certain. Still she hesitated. 'Accept them, *tesoro*. If you don't, then no one else will ever get the chance. I shall take them back home unopened, and straight into the river Arno they go.'

His eyes were warm with all the feeling she had seen there in his unguarded moments. This must be another one. Hardly daring to hope, she lifted one hand a fraction.

Then she stopped. Gianni lowered his chin and slowly raised his eyebrows, encouraging her silently.

Her fingers automatically went towards the smallest present. Gianni moved as though to stop her, hesitated, but then decided that he couldn't leave well alone even now.

'No—don't take that one. Open this one first.'

She said nothing, but the look on her face as she accepted a different red velvet parcel told Gianni all he wanted to know.

'Believe me, it's not another example of me dictating to you. There is a reason why you should open these in a special order.'

He was moving uncomfortably under her scrutiny, and his voice was as close to apologetic as a man like Gianni was likely to get. Meg almost smiled, but couldn't bear to hurt his feelings.

Pulling open the fine gold ribbon, she unwrapped a battered leather case. It so obviously contained jewellery; she looked up at him in alarm.

'This must be one of the only occasions when a woman says "you shouldn't have" and means it from the bottom of her heart. Oh, Gianni, what have you done?'

'Open it, and see.'

His gaze was steady and level, but she could see a pulse in his neck. It was flickering almost as fast as her heart.

Obediently she dropped her gaze and concentrated on the small golden catch fastening the jewel case. The lid sprang open to reveal an extravagance of diamonds nestled in a bed of red velvet.

'It's a tiara.'

As quick as a flash Gianni lifted it out and set it on her hair.

'It feels funny...' she said with a puzzled smile.

'You'll get used to it.'

'No…no, I can't…I mustn't…'

Raising one hand to the gold and diamond crown, Meg tried to take it off. Gianni's hand met hers and held it there, in place on her head.

'Do you recognise it?'

'It looks like the coronet your mother was wearing in that portrait of your parents hanging in your suite.'

With his hand enfolding hers, Meg had no intention of struggling but she was worried. Her eyes flickered nervously over the little lemon tree. She was trying to remember exactly what else the *contessa* had been wearing in that frighteningly glamorous painting. As well as the coronet she had been draped in earrings, a necklace, a bracelet, rings…Meg racked her brains, wondering if there had been a wristwatch, too. That was the only thing she might have considered accepting, but nothing decorating the little tree looked remotely run-of-the-mill.

'I can't wear this,' she repeated.

'It's for you. It's *all* for you,' Gianni said quietly. Presenting her with a second, smaller package, he released her hand to let her unwrap it. Inside an antique case was a pair of stunning earrings to match the tiara. A waterfall of rose-cut diamonds fell from a fine filigree of eighteen-carat gold lace. Meg knew she couldn't possibly take them. These exquisite trinkets were exactly the sort of prizes awarded to women like Thomas Hardy's 'Ruined Maid'. Mistresses. If she fell under Gianni's spell again she would be lost for ever. He would trample over her heart, her life would never be her own and all the diamonds in the world could never restore her self-respect.

She could hardly find the words to speak. 'These are the

most beautiful earrings I have ever seen,' she breathed eventually. 'But I can't possibly accept them—or any of these lovely things!'

'I'll put them on for you,' he said, moving forward quickly. Before she could refuse, he silenced her with a look. Lifting the first earring out of its red velvet bed, he fastened it expertly into her lobe. Soon he had fixed the second network of precious stones to her other ear. 'If you can't wear them, Meg, then no other woman in the history of the world is going to have the benefit of them. I mean that. They're yours. You're entitled to them.'

She gazed up at him, her eyes troubled. 'Gianni, you owe me nothing. That's what I said, and I meant it.'

'Are you sure?' He looked at her uncertainly.

It was the first time Meg had seen him wear an expression other than supreme self-confidence. Suddenly she was scared. Her world had started spinning out of control when she'd discovered she was pregnant. The only dependable thing left in her universe was Gianni's certainty. To discover that was no longer set in stone terrified her. They couldn't both be adrift in wild, uncharted waters. Desperately, Meg tried to restore the natural order of things. When she delivered her bombshell, he would bounce back to furious normal.

'Look—Gianni—I thought nothing could ever tear this secret out of me, but you're forcing my hand…'

Instantly all the old Bellini pride returned. Gianni drew himself up and regarded her with hooded eyes. Meg took a deep, steadying breath. She had spent hours dreading his fury, planning her defence and going over and over what she would say. Now the moment was here, she felt strangely calm. Reliving every possible way he might explode had prepared her for the very worst. It had convinced her she could cope. After all, an angry Gianni was far less scary than the man who stood before her now, trying unsuccessfully to hide shadows of doubt.

'You need to know exactly how little all your wealth and possessions mean to me, Gianni? Well, I'll tell you.' Her palms were damp. She clenched her fists. Gianni's eyes darted to the movement, then up to her face. His suspicion stiffened her nerves. This was the man she knew—tough, uncompromising—a lone wolf if ever there was one. *With all the emphasis on the word lone*, she thought nervously.

'The truth is, Gianni…I loved working on the Castelfino Estate, and making the decision to leave was so hard…so very hard, I don't know how I survived.' She took a deep, noisy breath, bracing herself to put the awful truth into words. Her hand automatically went to her waist again, reminding herself of her new responsibility. 'I would soon have swallowed my pride and tried to get my job back. But now there's something stopping me, Gianni.'

He stared at her until the pulse throbbing in her veins rang through her head.

'Don't tell me—I know what you're going to say. You fell in love with me. When all I did was to tell you—and myself—over and over again that I didn't want any emotional ties?'

Unable to bear his scrutiny any longer, she closed her eyes and shook her head.

'No, it's not that.' Through all her pain she heard him take a sharp breath.

'I find it *very* hard to believe you didn't fall in love with me,' he said indignantly.

All Meg's tensions exploded in laughter.

'Oh, Gianni! Only you could say something like that at

a time like this! Of course I fell in love with you! That was the main reason I had to get away. I loved you, but you could never love me. When I found out you didn't even respect me, well, that was the end. And then when I discovered I was pregnant—'

She stopped with a squeak of horror. After all her careful build-up, the word escaped by accident. She was as shocked by her simple revelation as Gianni was. She had been mentally mapping out all sorts of complicated ways of breaking the news a little bit at a time. In the end, it popped out all by itself.

They stared at each other until finally Gianni broke the spell and looked away.

'I—I don't know what to say.'

He really didn't. Meg could see the truth of his words in the way his shoulders sagged momentarily as he absorbed the body blow she had delivered.

'Oh—no—this isn't how it's supposed to be!' she wailed. 'I've hurt you, and I never meant to! I didn't ever expect to see you again, so I thought I'd never need to tell you—that's why it happened like this! I should have taken more time to explain—oh, no, this is horrible—' Meg was gabbling, perspiring, gesticulating and crying but Gianni's response froze her instantly.

'No…no, it isn't,' he said slowly. 'Don't blame yourself, Meg. It takes two to make a baby. Although when it can have happened I have no idea…' He let her go and reached for one of the dining chairs. Pulling it away from the table, he lowered her gently into it.

'You shouldn't be standing—not in your condition,' he murmured. Planting his hands on either side of her, he looked deep into her eyes. She waited in awestruck silence.

'I've been fooling myself for too long. Deep down, all the parties, the girls, the excesses—it was all a hopeless search for love. When you walked into my life I started seeing things differently, Meg, but not clearly enough. On the night of the banquet my body spoke, not my mind. It cried out for you in the only way it knew you could never resist. A long-term commitment was something I didn't want to get mixed up with. At the time.' There was total certainty in his voice now. As he gazed into her eyes all Meg's doubts disappeared.

'Then…you don't mind about the baby?'

Leaning forward, he rested his brow against hers.

'My love, it is what I've always wanted—although it took you to make me realise it. I want to give my child all the love I never experienced when I was growing up. If you walk away from me now, we'll all lose out. All three of us.'

'I wouldn't…I couldn't…no, what I mean is—I want you, and this baby, more than anything I've ever wanted in my life, Gianni. But I can't be your mistress any more. I would have kept the baby a secret if we hadn't met up again today—and what will your fiancée say?' Meg flustered.

'I don't know. What *do* you say, Meg?' Gianni smiled, silencing her with a feather-light kiss. There was no resisting him, and Meg didn't want to. For a long time they were suspended in delicious silence. 'I want you now more than ever. I owe all the happiness that these past weeks have brought me to you. You warmed my heart as beautifully as you warmed my bed.' His voice became a low murmur as he buried his face in her hair, but Meg couldn't relinquish her last finger hold on respectability without a fight.

'I can't do this, Gianni. Really, I can't. My skin isn't thick enough. I can't go on being your mistress, and I can't bear to think of you marrying another woman. Imagine how much more painful it will be for me to become nothing more than a bystander in your life. I'll be sidelined in favour of your wife, and over the years as your legitimate children are born and grow, my baby and I will be pushed further and further away from you. We'll be abandoned and forgotten—'

'It isn't going to be like that.' His voice resonated through her entire body.

'But it will be! It *will*!' In a sudden panic Meg tried to pull away from him.

In the stillness of the dining room her priceless antique jewellery tinkled, the candlelight sending brightly coloured stars dancing in a halo around her head.

'No, it won't. I won't let it. Listen to me, Meg!'

'I've listened to you too often in the past, Gianni. This is hopeless! I can't be your mistress any longer!'

'I know!' he barked, silencing her instantly. Once her full attention was riveted on him he spoke with a quiet authority that almost stopped her heart.

'I want you to become my *wife*, Meg,' he explained slowly. 'I want you as my *contessa* as well as my lover. My partner. My companion. My *friend*,' he finished softly.

It took Meg several seconds to realise what she was hearing.

'But what about—' She looked across at the table set for two, crowned by the beautiful flower she had brought for presentation to Gianni's fiancée.

'Bellini men don't beg,' he said succinctly. 'The moment I saw you again today I knew I had to have you, and you alone, Meg. Now and for ever. I had the Bellini hoard wrapped and flown over especially, in time for your arrival tonight. I love you, Meg, and without you I'm only one half of the spectacular whole our family will be.'

There were no fanfares and no fireworks. Gianni simply spoke all the words she had longed to hear. It felt like coming home, without ever having been away. Slowly, delicately she leaned forward until her head was resting against his chest. She expected to feel the slow, steady beat of his heart. It would have been perfectly in accord with the indulgent way he silently stroked her hair and patted her shoulders. Instead, she got a surprise. A rapid pulse thrummed through his body in feverish excitement.

'Can I trust you, Gianni?' she whispered.

'With our baby's life,' he assured her, kissing the crown of her head with its sparkle of diamonds. Meg melted as he pressed the side of his face against hers. For a long time she sheltered in his arms, trying to catch her breath as she thought back over the pain of the last days. All she had ever wanted was to feel safe and secure in Gianni's love. Now she had a promise, and trinkets beyond her wildest dreams, but none of it meant anything at all without integrity. A single tear beaded her lashes and rolled down her cheek. His face pressed tightly against hers, Gianni felt it the moment it fell. Alarmed, he straightened up and held her at arm's length, studying her intently.

'You're crying!' He could hardly believe it. 'What's the matter? I only wanted to make you happy!'

'D-did you?' Blinded with tears, Meg gazed at him in hopeless doubt. 'If that's the case, w-why did you spend all that time keeping me at arm's length? Y-you never even put my details on your phone!' she sobbed, almost inaudibly. Chuckling, Gianni drew her towards him again.

'That's because I never needed to. They're here,' he

said softly, lifting her hand and pressing her palm against his chest. 'Every word you have ever spoken to me is carved in my heart, Meg.'

She felt it beating more slowly and steadily beneath her fingers. Gianni closed his fingers around hers and took them to his lips for a gentle kiss.

'Really?' she whispered.

'Really.' He nodded. 'Meg, my love, you are the only woman for me, now and for ever. I'm going to take you as my wife, my mistress and my soulmate. From the moment we met no woman has matched up to you in any way. I spent my whole life looking for love, but in all the wrong places. And when we found each other, I almost let you slip through my fingers. That's never going to happen again. I can promise you that.'

She leaned against him. He gathered her in to his body. Once upon a time Meg would have been terrified to admit she wanted someone she could depend on. Now she was safe in Gianni's arms, she could see things so much more clearly. He needed her every bit as much as she needed him. They were a team now. It didn't matter which one of them dealt with the little niggles and worries of day-to-day life, as long as they were solved.

As though reading her mind he held her close and whispered: 'I never thought I would find a woman I could rely on. You are all I need, my love. You—and our family,' he said simply, before his kisses swept her away to a place where nothing else mattered any more.

HARLEQUIN *Presents*

Coming Next Month

in **Harlequin Presents®**. Available July 27, 2010.

Coming Next Month

in **Harlequin Presents® EXTRA**. Available August 10, 2010.

HPECNM0710

LARGER-PRINT BOOKS!

HARLEQUIN *Presents~*

PASSION GUARANTEED SEDUCTION

GET 2 FREE LARGER-PRINT NOVELS PLUS 2 FREE GIFTS!

HPLP10R

HARLEQUIN®

A *Romance*

FOR EVERY MOOD™

Spotlight on
Heart & Home

Heartwarming romances
where love can happen
right when you least expect it.

See the next page to enjoy a sneak peek
from Harlequin® American Romance®,
a Heart and Home series.

Five hunky Texas single fathers—five stories from Cathy Gillen Thacker's LONE STAR DADS *miniseries. Here's an excerpt from the latest,* THE MOMMY PROPOSAL *from Harlequin American Romance.*

"I hear you work miracles," Nate Hutchinson drawled. Brooke Mitchell had just stepped into his lavishly appointed office in downtown Fort Worth, Texas.

"Sometimes, I do." Brooke smiled and took the sexy financier's hand in hers, shook it briefly.

"Good." Nate looked her straight in the eye. "Because I'm in need of a home makeover—fast. The son of an old friend is coming to live with me."

She was still tingling from the feel of his warm palm. "Temporarily or permanently?"

"If all goes according to plan, I'll adopt Landry by summer's end."

Brooke had heard the founder of Nate Hutchinson Financial Services was eligible, wealthy and generous to a fault. She hadn't known he was in the market for a family, but she supposed she shouldn't be surprised. But Brooke had figured a man as successful and handsome as Nate would want one the old-fashioned way. *Not that this was any of her business...*

"So what's the child like?" she asked crisply, trying not to think how the marine-blue of Nate's dress shirt deepened the hue of his eyes.

"I don't know." Nate took a seat behind his massive antique mahogany desk. He relaxed against the smooth leather of the chair. "I've never met him."

"Yet you've invited this kid to live with you permanently?"

"It's complicated. But I'm sure it's going to be fine."

Obviously Nate Hutchinson knew as little about teenage

boys as he did about decorating. But that wasn't her problem. Finding a way to do the assignment without getting the least bit emotionally involved was.

Find out how a young boy brings Nate and Brooke together in THE MOMMY PROPOSAL, coming August 2010 from Harlequin American Romance.

HAREXP0810

THE HEAT IS ON

by

Jill Shalvis

The attraction between Bella and
Detective Madden is undeniable.
But can a few wild encounters
turn into love?

Don't miss this hot read.

*Available in August
where books are sold.*

A powerful dynasty, eight daughters in disgrace…

Absolute scandal has rocked the core of the infamous
Balfour family. The glittering, gorgeous daughters are in
disgrace…. Banished from the Balfour mansion, they're
sent to the boldest, most magnificent men
to be wedded, bedded…and tamed!

And so begins a scandalous saga of dazzling glamour
and passionate surrender.

Beginning August 2010

8 volumes to collect and treasure!
